VAMPIRE ROYALS 1: THE PAGEANT

LEIGH WALKER

CMG PUBLISHING

Published by CMG Publishing.

Cover by Melody Simmons.

Sign up for Leigh's mailing list at **www.leighwalkerbooks.com**.

Created with Vellum

CHAPTER 1
THE FIFTH WEDDING

"YOU'RE NOT SUPPOSED TO DRESS LIKE THAT AT A WEDDING." Lyra looked at me in disapproval. "All your pieces and bits are hanging out. You're supposed to be here in support of our friend."

I leaned toward Lyra. "My mother made me wear this," I whispered. I adjusted the bodice of my tight-fitting gown, but nothing could stop me from spilling out of it. "She thinks they're watching us and every public outing is an opportunity to win points."

Lyra rolled her eyes. "Your mother is disgusting. I can't believe she wants you to enter that thing and marry that filthy beast!"

I sighed. "She's ambitious. She also doesn't like starving."

"Who does? Just pull that thing *up*, Gwyn."

I grimaced and pulled the dress up. Lyra had a point. The female guests around me were covered from their necks to their wrists. This was the fifth wedding I'd attended in as many weeks. I should know better.

I *did* know better, and so did my mother. But she wanted

me to get invited to the Pageant, and I didn't want her and my younger siblings to die of malnutrition.

I shivered, cutting off the thought, and turned my gaze toward the front of the old-fashioned church. It was one of the few that remained from before the Great War. The stained glass above the pulpit was miraculously intact. The late-afternoon sun splashed through, splaying multicolored lights across the gleaming wooden floor.

The groom, adolescent acne flaring across his cheeks, nervously adjusted his suit as the music began to play.

Tavi, my friend since childhood, took her first halting steps down the aisle. She looked beautiful in her white lace dress, but her skin was pale, and her eyes were wild beneath her veil. Her hand shook, and her father grasped it, urging her forward.

Tavi barely knew her fiancé. She'd first met him three weeks ago.

Lyra frowned then crossed herself. "Here we go again."

"How was the ceremony?" my mother asked. She poured a thin soup into my bowl.

I scowled at the watery broth. One lone carrot sank hopelessly toward the bottom. "Awkward. Tavi looked petrified."

My mother snorted then remembered herself. She smoothed her complexion into its usual mask of attractive superiority. "Tavi *should* be petrified. That boy is a bony disaster. Her parents spent every last dime on that stupid wedding, as if it's going to help anything. The only thing that boy will give her is a baby they won't be able to feed."

"It might be better than the alternative."

Mom scoffed. "Really, Gwyneth? Being a princess is a worse fate?"

I put down my spoon. "You've seen the prince, right? And heard all the stories about him and his family?" A rhetorical question. My mother knew all about how King and Queen Black, together with their one son, had come down from the North to "save" the settlements. The tale had been shoved down our throats every day since they'd conquered us.

My older brother, Balkyn, and my father had never come back from the Great War. And still, my mother was oh-so-eager to marry me off to the prince. *Ridiculous.*

"Mommy!" my younger sister, Winifred, screeched from the living room. "It's on. Come quick!"

I groaned and followed my mother to the television. It was the only electronic device that still worked, and that was because the government wanted it that way.

Winifred and my younger brother, Remy, were seated next to each other on the love seat. I ruffled Remy's hair as he clutched his blanket, his wide eyes fixed on the screen.

"They're talking about the contest." Winifred arranged her stuffed animals next to her so they could watch. "Do you think they'll show the prince?"

"They always show the prince, Winnie." I stoked the fire then flopped down on the floor in front of my siblings, pulling my knees toward my chest. I eyed the wood supply, which was low again. My mother used the logs too quickly, and Winnie and Remy didn't understand. They only felt the cold and wanted comfort. I would have to go out for more wood tomorrow and scold them all about using it sparingly.

The prince's official image flashed on the screen, handsome and foreboding. *The Dark Prince.* That was what we all called him, a name we would never say in public. He wore a long black robe and a gleaming crown. He cut an impressive figure with his square jaw and broad shoulders, as if he'd been born into nobility instead of having slaughtered his way into it. His sable eyes shone out of his stony but striking face.

"He's so handsome. I wish I could marry him." Winnie sighed. She was only eight and didn't remember the war.

"He's scary." Remy hid under his blanket.

I agreed with Remy, but I kept my mouth shut lest my mother smack me upside the head.

"Shh." Mom settled herself between my brother and sister just as the image faded and the update began.

"The news you've all been waiting for is finally here," the narrator said. "Please stay tuned for an official broadcast." The images on the screen showed the royal family—the king, the queen, and the prince—waving to adoring onlookers at a midnight parade. *Propaganda.* Then there was a group of young women wearing gowns, eagerly smiling as a long line of paparazzi took pictures of them. The last image was of a young woman kneeling, a crown being placed on her head.

The promotional sequence panned out, and Mira Kinney, the government-sanctioned television personality, smiled out at us from her news desk. Her blond bob was impeccable, as was her smooth skin, red sheath, and white, even teeth.

"This just in, fellow settlers—the Pageant has officially begun. The contest is law. Rollout begins immediately. Contestants will be notified of their invitation beginning tonight at midnight. That's right—*tonight*."

My mother put a hand over her heart.

Mira checked her notes, or pretended to. I had a feeling she knew all the details of this story, the juiciest since the Great War. "All unmarried young women of age in the settlements—those aged seventeen and eighteen—were considered."

I swallowed hard. I'd just celebrated my eighteenth birthday last week.

Mira smiled broadly at the camera, flashing those teeth.

"The contestants for the Pageant have already been hand-picked. For those who've been lucky enough to be selected, participation is mandatory. This is an opportunity you don't say no to, ladies."

Can't say no to. That was what she meant.

"Every settlement in the land will be represented by two contestants. Fifty young ladies will be competing for the ultimate prize—an engagement to the prince."

My mother fanned herself. Winnie hugged her favorite bear. Remy sunk further under the blanket, and I wished I could join him.

Mira beamed at the camera. "Once the contestants have been notified, more details will be forthcoming. For now, wait for that doorbell to ring, settlers. It could mean the beginning of a *very* exciting future for your family."

CHAPTER 2
THE INVITATION

We all slept, or pretended to sleep, in the living room. Winter was coming, and we'd closed off the upstairs of our townhouse to conserve heat.

I watched the dying fire, trying not to pay attention to the time as it passed. I willed the doorbell not to ring.

I knew my mother was awake, but I ignored her. The last thing I wanted to hear was her conjecture about who would be picked from our settlement or, worse yet, her hope it would be me.

She had to hate the royal family as much as I did. She mourned Balkyn and my father, just like me. But our money was long gone, and the weekly rations from the government were insufficient. There was no work for either of us. The government had been reclassifying jobs and hiring the most qualified applicants first.

Before the war, my mother had been a stay-at-home mom, and I'd been a student. Neither of us was the most qualified for any of the government's super-competitive positions. I'd taken to hawking our family's knickknacks and china at the local black market, using the money or goods I received for firewood, milk, and bread.

At this rate, we weren't going to last long.

As if hearing my thoughts, my mother sat up. A lock of glossy auburn hair escaped her bun, and she tucked it behind her ear. "I know you think I'm a monster for hoping you'll be chosen." She kept her voice low, careful not to wake my brother and sister, who were curled up close to the fireplace.

"I don't." A lie.

"Don't pretend, Gwyneth. We shouldn't bother with civilities like that anymore."

I eyed her cashmere sweater and scoffed. "You seem pretty attached to your civilities."

She stroked the luxurious fabric of her sweater. "I miss our way of life. Who wouldn't?"

Before the war, my father had run a successful bond-trading business. I'd gone to private school and had riding lessons. Balkyn had attended a prestigious private college. Winnie and Remy had had a full-time nanny. My mother spent her days volunteering for various charities and sweating out imagined toxins at hot yoga, while one maid had cleaned our home and another one had stocked our refrigerator.

The dying embers gleamed in the fireplace. All that luxury seemed like such a waste, now.

"If I could do something to change our situation, I would." My mother squared her shoulders. "But I'm too old for pageants, and I haven't found someone suitable to...take care of us."

"You don't even know if Daddy's dead." My voice was low, but it shook. "You can't get remarried."

"It's been five years. I don't think he's coming back." She pulled the sweater close against her chest.

"You still can't—"

"I won't let my children starve," she snapped. "You're not a mother. You don't understand."

I watched Remy's chest rising and falling, Winifred snuggled against him for warmth. "I understand more than you think."

She shot me a quick look. "Then if you get selected—and Gwyneth, you are absolutely stunning, so you have a good chance—please try your best. Please don't be..."

Stubborn? Superior? Fresh? All the things she's accused me of being over the past five years?

"Difficult."

"I won't be. I didn't run off and elope, did I?" I'd thought about it. Drew Baylor, loyal to a fault, had even asked me if I wanted to. I'd turned him down. I had to take care of my family, and getting married at eighteen was *not* my idea of happily ever after.

And yet, if I somehow got invited to this godforsaken contest, that was exactly what I'd be fighting for. *To marry a filthy Northerner.*

"You heard what they said. The winner gets an engagement to the prince." I kept my voice low. "It could mean sanctuary for all of us."

She nodded, exhaling deeply. "I know. That's why I've been taking such pains with your appearance. I knew they'd be watching you and the other girls. You have a chance, a real chance." She checked the time. "You should get some rest. Tomorrow's going to be a long day."

"Mom, wait." I took a deep breath. "The odds aren't good, even if I *am* selected. We're going to run out of things to trade sooner rather than later. What... what are we going to do?"

My mother's dark-brown eyes glowed in the firelight. She

was so beautiful, but there was something fierce about her features, as if she might turn on you at any moment and make a designer handbag out of your hide.

She shrugged. "We'll think of something. We always do. We're Wests."

❧

I'd just fallen into a light sleep when the doorbell rang. I cracked one eye open as my mother scrambled for the door. Remy and Winnie didn't move, both in a deep slumber.

I looked at the clock. It was midnight.

I was cursed, born with my mother's good looks.

She spoke in low tones to whoever stood on the other side of the door. A large envelope was pressed into her hands, and then the courier was gone.

Mother clutched the envelope, beaming, and waved for me to meet her in the kitchen.

I obeyed, my legs heavy as lead.

Two hectic spots of color flushed her cheeks. "That was a sentinel."

"Obviously." I eyed the envelope. "What did he say?"

"You've been selected for the Pageant."

I sucked in a deep breath. "When does it begin?"

"Tomorrow morning." She put the envelope on the table. "We have to get you ready, Gwyn."

"Am I…leaving?"

She nodded then pushed the envelope toward me. "He said it was for you."

Shakily, I opened it, careful to avoid a paper cut. I didn't want to see blood. I didn't want to think about it, either, not where I was about to go.

I slid out the embossed letter, its fancy script printed carefully on parchment paper. Hands shaking, I clutched the message as I read.

Dear Ms. West,
Congratulations! After a search across the settlements, you have been selected as a contestant in The Pageant, representing Settlement 4.
The Committee has selected each participant on the basis of achievement, presentation, and a review of your academic and family history.
A government representative will come to collect you tomorrow morning at six a.m. Please be prepared. It's not necessary for you to pack any clothes or toiletries as these will be provided by The Royal Family. However, contestants are allowed to bring one small parcel with personal belongings.
The winner of The Pageant will be chosen by the Royal Family, including Prince Black and his committee. Contestants will be judged on their merits. The grand prize: an engagement to His Highness, to be followed by a royal wedding.
We look forward to getting to know you better over the coming weeks.
Sincerely,
King and Queen Black

I scoffed. I'd been picked on the basis of my family history? My family had fought to keep the Blacks at bay, to drive them and their shadowy supporters back to the North.

"What did it say?" My mother was breathless as I put the letter on the table.

"They're coming for me tomorrow morning at six. And I don't need to pack anything."

She watched me carefully. "What else?"

Our gazes locked across the table. "If I win, the prince will propose. And there'll be a royal wedding."

My mother crossed herself, something I'd never seen her do before.

"Why did you do that?"

Her dark eyes glittered, and she pursed her lips. "Because we're about to make a deal with the devil."

I shivered. "We don't know what they are, Mother. Not for sure."

She rummaged through a cupboard. "I thought we weren't pretending anymore." She brought out a bottle filled with amber liquid, poured two shots, and slid one into my hand.

"You're letting me have alcohol?" I sniffed the liquid, wincing as it burned my nose.

She clinked her glass against mine. "For courage."

I sighed. Courage was something I'd struggled with since the strange royal family had taken over our land and our lives. I'd tried to be brave and keep our family afloat, but I lived with fear every day—fear for my family's existence, fear that my father and Balkyn were never coming back, fear that my younger brother and sister were going to end up slaves.

And now, I was headed to the palace in the morning, to the home of the very people responsible for our predicament. *Courage, indeed.* "I'll drink to that."

My mother finished her shot quickly then sighed. "You're fortunate to be beautiful, Gwyn. That's why you were given this opportunity."

I frowned. "But it's ridiculous, isn't it?"

She nodded. "It is, indeed. Far better to be clever than beautiful, my mother always said."

"I couldn't agree more."

"Good thing you're both." Mother eyed me. "Your looks can't save you in the end. Only your wits can do that."

"I know." I grimaced. "I'll do what I can to win. I know what it would mean for our family." I'd rather stick a hot poker in my eye and eat spiders than marry the prince, but I wasn't in a position to be picky.

When he'd left for the war, I'd promised my father I'd take care of the family. I would give my life to keep that promise. He'd done as much for me.

Mom's gaze held mine. "Good girl. Do your best, but never forget where you came from. Never forget who you are, and never, ever let yourself forget who *they* are."

"They're the reason Daddy and Balkyn are gone. I could never forget."

"Your father told me something before he left, something I should pass on to you."

I put the glass down without drinking, which I'd heard was bad luck, but at this point, what could it matter? "I'm listening."

She put her hands on my shoulders and faced me. "You are a West, and that means you're a survivor. You're going to make it through this. I know you will."

"It's a beauty pageant, Mom, not a prison camp."

She arched an eyebrow. "It might be more cutthroat than you think. The competition's going to be fierce."

My stomach flipped. "You think it will be…dangerous?" I'd thought it would be boring and sort of posh, a bunch of girls sitting around on velvet couches and eating tarts.

"You haven't seen a lot of the world. I blame myself and your father. He wanted you all to grow up in a bubble. Safe, happy, protected. You don't know how brutal the world can be, Gwyn. The royal family are creatures of the night, and the settlements are starving. Every girl in this competition is going to be fighting for their lives, for their family's lives. Of course, it's going to be dangerous. You'll be surrounded by people trying to knock you down or elbow you out of the way, darling. Or worse."

I decided to try the drink. The tiny sip burned as it worked its way down my throat.

"Back to what your father told me. Being a West means being a survivor, but sometimes surviving is the worst thing. It means you live through terrible times and see things you wish you could unsee. You'll live to see your friends and family suffer. But you're a West, and that means you don't give up, and you don't get to roll over and hide your eyes. So if something bad happens during the next few weeks, speak up. Stand up for what you believe. But for the love of all things holy, stay alive."

I had more of the drink. The burning in my throat distracted me from the throb in my head. "Why are they doing this? I'm sure the prince could have any girl he wanted. They brought thousands of them down from the North."

"But those aren't human girls, and they aren't settlers. The royal family is smarter than that. It's been five years, and we still haven't accepted the new government. They must know the settlements are planning a revolt. This is their way of binding us to them, one of our own becoming a princess. One of our own to someday become the queen and rule over the settlements."

I nodded. "It's a way to appease us, to make us feel like we're their equal."

"All while keeping us enslaved, waiting on our rations, our men dead or imprisoned." My mother fingered the necklace my father had given her, a solitary diamond on a gold chain. She would have to sell it soon. And probably do things a lot worse than that.

"Do you think they're still alive? Daddy and Balkyn?"

"Sometimes at night, I think I can feel him or hear him and your brother, but it's only the wind. If they've gone on, I know it's to a better place. But we aren't ready to join them, Gwyn." She smiled and tapped me on the chin. "Not just yet."

CHAPTER 3
GIRL ON THE TRAIN

AT EXACTLY SIX THE NEXT MORNING, OUR DOORBELL RANG. Winnie and Remy still slept soundly on the floor. I'd decided not to wake them to say goodbye. I didn't want them to cry, or worse, to panic.

I was trying to keep panic at bay.

Plus, I was pretty sure I'd be the one to break down.

The silent sentinel waited as I buttoned my coat and my mother fussed over me. She smoothed my hair and kissed my forehead. "Please write to me as soon as you get there. Let me know everything, Gwyneth."

"I will, Mother. I promise. Tell Tavi and Lyra what happened, okay? Tell them I'll write. And please tell Remy and Winnie I love them. Tell Winnie I'll get the prince's autograph for her."

My mother beamed, but dark circles bloomed like bruises beneath her eyes. The sentinel cleared his throat. *Time to go.*

My throat closed up. "I love you." I glanced back at my brother and sister, fear gnawing at me. For some reason, I worried I'd never see them again.

It's just a beauty pageant, not a prison camp.

"Wait a minute," I told the sentinel and rushed to the living room. I kissed the top of Remy's head, then Winnie's.

Winnie swatted at me. "Gwyn, stop."

"You little nerdlings need to know something. I love you. Be good for Mother. Help her with the wood." I nodded at Remy. "You keep track of the logs, and make sure to note when we're running low. I'm counting on you."

His eyes were huge. "Okay."

"I love you." I kissed his cheeks, then Winnie's. Wiping the tears from my face, I nodded at my mother.

Then I followed the sentinel out into the freezing, silent morning.

He didn't say a word as his boots crunched over the frosty earth. His uniform was gray flannel, warm and functional. It looked new and immaculately pressed.

The sun started to rise in the east, a pinkish hue surrounding it. I peered at the guard. He didn't look concerned. He was human, then.

I wasn't so sure about the rest of them. The royal family only made appearances after the sun had set. During the Great War, the royal guard had staged all of their attacks against the settlements at night.

Although the guard hadn't spoken, I found enough nerve to ask him a question. "Where are you from?"

"The city." His accent was flat, familiar.

"How'd they get you to work for them?" I blurted out. It was probably the only chance he had at a regular paycheck, but still. He was human and from here. I hadn't realized our kind worked for them.

He looked at me sharply. "You're not allowed to talk to any males except for the prince and the royal emissary unless one of us asks you a direct question," the guard said quickly. "Don't say another word to me."

I didn't. I bit my lip instead.

We passed the golden Joan of Arc, one of the city's few remaining statues, a reminder of our settlement's former glory. Silently, the guard led me to the train station, his face pale and stoic as we waited for the train. I'd never ridden a train before. When I was in school, a hired car had taken me to the academy and to my private lessons. Now, I walked everywhere I needed to go. Before the war, only workers had used the trains. Now, no one used it except for the government.

I held my breath as a train approached, metal wheels squealing against the tracks. I obediently followed the guard aboard, clutching my lone bag of possessions. The doors closed behind us, and before I was ready, the train jerked to life. I had to scramble into a nearby seat before I fell flat on my face.

"Awkward." The girl in the seat next to mine admired her nail polish, not looking up. "I like it."

"I'm sorry?" The guard stood nearby, but he didn't correct me for speaking to the girl.

She eyed me from beneath her strawberry-blond curls. "I said you're awkward. And that I liked it."

The girl, although rude, was very pretty. She must be another contestant. "I'm...Gwyneth." I held out my hand. "Gwyneth West, Settlement Four."

She eyed my hand until I gave up and dropped it into my lap.

"I'm Eve. Settlement Four as well."

"I've never seen you before." I was surprised. Our settlement was one of the smaller ones, and I'd assumed the other contestant would be from my school or one of the other elite academies.

"That's because they went slumming for me." She smiled without warmth. "I'm from the projects."

"Oh." I racked my brain for something appropriate to say to the bristly girl.

Her aqua eyes flicked over me. "I know you're from the Upper East End. You don't have to talk to me."

"Uh... I might not talk to you because you're a *jerk*, but I could care less where you live."

A small smile tugged at the outer edges of her lips. She held out her hand. "Eve Whitely, unwilling and ungrateful contestant in the Pageant."

My guard's eyes widened at her boldness. Her guard shifted away, as if she might be contagious.

I leaned forward. "Let's talk more about that later, shall we? What school did you go to?" I deftly changed the subject, my mother's years of social training kicking in.

"The slum school. I take it you went to the Upper Academy?"

I nodded. "Have you met any of the other girls?"

She shook her head. "Rusty here"—she motioned to the guard next to her, who had red hair—"said we aren't allowed to mingle with the girls from the other settlements. Not until we get there."

I licked my lips. "Do you know where we're going?"

"The palace, I'm guessing." Eve shrugged. "Where else are they going to lock us all up?"

I coughed and gave her a warning look. "I'm sure they won't need to do that. It's just a beauty pageant, after all."

"Just a beauty pageant, huh?" Eve leaned back against her seat, all lazy confidence. "You have *met* other girls before, haven't you?"

"Yes, but—"

"Not to mention that the prince and his stiff parents are filthy bloodsuckers. My money says they'll be locking us up ASAP."

I coughed, spluttering a bit. My mother had been right. I'd been raised in a bubble. I'd never heard someone speak so brazenly before. Even the other traders at the black market wouldn't dare.

Eve grinned, a rogue's smile. "Just saying."

The prince and his stiff parents are filthy bloodsuckers.

I opened my mouth to respond then snapped it shut. Because really, what could I say to *that*?

CHAPTER 4
A HINT OF TROUBLE

AFTER SOME TIME PASSED, THE TRAIN SCREECHED TO A HALT. I peered out the window to see another gray train station. On the platform were two well-dressed girls and their guards. The girls fidgeted, waiting for the doors to open. They got into another compartment, and the train sped off again.

Over the next few hours, we made several more stops. The passing landscape told me we were heading south. The light dusting of snow disappeared, replaced with greener and greener grass.

I knew the girls in the western settlements were being collected a different way. The trains didn't run out there. I wondered what the other contestants were like and if any of them were as wild and outspoken as Eve.

I also wondered just how thoroughly the royal family had checked our backgrounds.

Eve ignored me, humming to herself and watching the landscape fly by. There wasn't much we could say in front of the guards, anyway.

Another hour passed, and there was a knock on the interior door of our train car. "Food service."

The guards opened the door, and an older woman, also wearing a gray uniform, came through. *Another human servant.* She wheeled a cart laden with sandwiches and fruit. Eve's eyeballs almost popped out of her head as she examined the feast. My stomach roared as the woman bowed to us and smiled kindly. "Tea?"

"Yes, please."

Eve nodded, her eyes never leaving the food. I heard her stomach rumble and looked at her with sympathy.

"Don't." Her voice was quiet. "Pity's the last thing I need. A sandwich is the first."

I tried to consume my food in a ladylike fashion, but it was *so* good, better than I'd had in years. Soon enough, I was gobbling my second sandwich of roast turkey and brie. Eve grabbed a third and groaned when she could only finish half. "I can't fit anymore, which really pisses me off, to be honest."

I giggled. I had no trouble finishing mine.

My stomach full for the first time in forever, I must've fallen asleep, because I was startled awake by the train screeching again. Eve clapped my shoulder. "We're here. Time to face the, er…music." She winked at me and made fake fangs with her fingers.

I would've laughed at her boldness, but I suddenly felt sick to my stomach. Time to face the music, indeed.

Eve was the first one who'd ever said it out loud in front of me. *Filthy bloodsuckers.* As if it were a fact, universally acknowledged. As if everyone would know what she meant when she made finger fangs.

Eve thought the royals were vampires. *Was it true?* My mother had never admitted it, but I knew that was why my father and brother had gone off to fight—to protect us from them, from their kind.

I'd known they were different, but I didn't know they were *that* different. Not for sure.

My mind raced. The king's and queen's appearances were always made under cover of darkness. The Black Guard only struck against us at night.

I fell in line behind Eve, my own guard close at my heels. I wished I could ask him what *he* knew, but I remembered what he'd said—no talking to men. So close to the palace, I didn't dare risk getting caught.

Fear flared through me as we exited the train. I smoothed my heavy travel dress and arranged my long, intricate braids. My mother had insisted I look my best while staying warm. Eve watched me and rolled her eyes. Now that she was standing, I noticed her casual pants tucked into combat boots and her coat, thin and cheaply made. It was only twenty degrees. She must have been freezing, but she didn't complain. She just scowled as I applied more lip gloss, as if I were ridiculous.

This southern train station was different, more stately and ornate. Black family royal crests adorned the walls. The crests were intricately carved and spectacularly colored with hues of purple, red, and the deepest blue. "This way, ladies." Eve's guard motioned for us to follow. "No talking."

I peered curiously at the other girls getting off the train. There were redheads and blondes, and girls with long dark hair artfully arranged like mine. There was straight hair, wavy hair, and curls. The girls were all manner of skin color and height. Some wore beautifully made clothes, and others wore hand-me-downs. There were skinny girls and curvy girls, and every size in between. *Did the prince have a type?*

I peered at their faces. Of the thirty girls I counted, the only thing they had in common was their beauty.

Eve eyed the competition too. "I guess the prince doesn't care for the homely ones. His harem, his rules, I guess."

Her guard's face reddened. "That's enough," he hissed.

She jauntily tossed her curls. "Easy, Rusty. Don't act so emotional and *human*. You might find yourself on the royal family's menu."

He looked as if he bit back a curse, but to his credit, he kept his mouth shut.

We filed out of the station, up a set of concrete stairs, and out to an open-air piazza. I inhaled the cold, fresh air gratefully, relishing the sun on my face after the long day of traveling. A tall guard, elegant and austere in a black coat with gold lapels, strode to the front of the group.

He cleared his throat. "Good afternoon, ladies. I'm General Isaacs." His white goatee gleamed in the late-afternoon sun. "Transportation will be here shortly to take us to our final destination. Please, no talking, and absolutely no photography. We'll have a meeting once we're safely inside. Stay with your settlement guards."

"Is he kidding about the photography?" Eve asked under her breath. "Does he think any of us still have cell phones?"

Once a taken-for-granted staple for every teenaged girl, the cell phone had gone the way of the dinosaur. Or rather, the government had collected them all and had them incinerated.

I shrugged in response. The general had said no talking, and although I didn't want to put Eve off, I wanted to follow instructions. He was close enough to hear us.

She sneered at me. "Oh, I see how it is. Upper East Side goody-two-shoes and all."

"Shut up," I whispered, and General Isaacs stiffened.

"When I said no talking, I meant it." He didn't have to raise his voice for icicles to jab at my spine. "We'll discuss how the rules are enforced at the meeting, but you should know that I am not kidding, and you will obey me."

Eve frowned at him. "Filthy bloodsucker lover." She said it under her breath, but I still heard her.

"What was that, young lady?" The general stared her down, his face a smooth, deadly mask.

Fear thrummed through me.

The row of girls in front of us parted, leaving a clear path to Eve. She squared her shoulders. "I said—"

I reached out and snatched her arm, squeezing. "She was just telling me what time it was, sir."

"Is that so?" General Isaacs crossed his arms against his powerful chest, waiting for Eve to respond.

"No, it is *not* so." Eve's breathing was loud, her nostrils flared. "I said you're a filthy—"

I stepped on her foot. Hard.

"Ow!"

The general strode toward us. The other girls backed up, frightened. "You two will be riding with me."

I forced myself to nod, conciliatory. "Yes, sir."

To her credit, Eve said absolutely nothing. But her jaw was tight, as if she were fighting hard to bite back words that were dying to spew forth.

I put my hand back on her arm, gently this time. *Easy,* I tried to say with my touch.

General Isaacs stayed nearby. Up close, I could see the moisture from his nostrils splayed across the top of his mustache. *Disgusting.*

He stared at me, his eyes a cold, brilliant blue. I shivered, and it had nothing to do with the cold. *And dangerous.*

We heard horses approaching, and a line of carriages pulled up to the curb. I looked at them with wonder as the other girls quietly murmured amongst themselves. *Horses. Real horses!* The government had confiscated them all when they took over. I used to ride every day, but these were the first horses I'd seen in years.

The general motioned for us to follow him to the first carriage, and our guards trailed behind. Even Eve looked impressed by the stately black coach and the team of beautiful white mares attached to the front. A young, handsome officer, dressed finely in the colors of the Black Court, opened the door to the coach for us. The driver tipped his shiny hat in our direction.

I made a mental note to discuss the sheer volume of human guards they had with Eve later. I was shocked. I'd thought only the Northerners worked for the royal family and the Black Guard. Apparently, I'd been wrong. At this one gathering, there were close to forty civilian guards.

I filed the information away for safekeeping as I climbed aboard the carriage.

The door closed behind us, and Eve and I sat silently as the general settled himself on the opposite bench. Our guards sat on either side of him, their faces grim.

The coachman flicked the reins, and the horses cantered off. Fields of green grass stretched out before us. It had already snowed lightly back home, but it was warmer here.

"Ladies." The general's low voice startled me. "We didn't get off to a good start. I'm sorry I singled you out, but it's my job to maintain order. I had to set an example."

I nodded once in acknowledgment, relieved. Eve said nothing, her silence stony.

The general's face softened. "Come now. I meant the apology. I can only imagine what you were saying back there, and trust me, I've heard it all." He smiled at Eve, the corners of his eyes crinkling. Had I just thought him disgusting? His smile transformed his face, making him look like a kindly, good-natured grandfather.

"You must be nervous, with the invitations coming just last night, and now, all this." He gestured out toward the fields just as soaring gates made of pristine gray stone came into view.

"Is this the palace?" I asked breathlessly.

He smiled in encouragement. "Yes, yes. Just wait until you see it up close. It's even more beautiful than it looks in the propaganda shorts."

My breath hitched. He'd said "propaganda." Was that an invitation to speak freely?

Eve leaned forward. I'd only met her hours before, but the smile on her face looked false. "Is the prince here? Will we meet him now?"

"Oh, yes," the General said. "He's thrilled the contest is finally getting started. It was his idea, you know."

Eve's aqua eyes were wide. "It was his idea to marry a civilian?"

"Absolutely. He's very forward-minded." The general nodded and smiled. "Are you excited to have been included, dear?"

The fake smile slid off Eve's face as she sat back, considering him. "Oh, I'm thrilled, *dear*."

My heart thudded in my ears. I willed her to shut up.

Eve continued. "I was thrilled with the sandwiches, so you might understand that I'm practically near tears to be so close to such *forward-minded greatness*."

The general sat back. "I think you'll be surprised by the prince."

Eve cocked her head at him. "I'm sure he's something, all right."

The smile slid from his face.

She elbowed me. "Did you hear that, Gwyn? The prince thinks mixing with us is cutting edge. I bet I get extra points for being a twofer—human *and* poor."

"Oh. Yes," I said stupidly. I blinked as I watched the hard stare on the General's face.

He glowered at Eve. "If you can't play along, you're going to find yourself in a tight spot. And like I said, you *will* obey me. You don't have a choice."

"But don't I? My mother always said—before she was killed by the Black Guard, that is—she said you always have a choice. And unlike you, I don't mind a bit of trouble, so long as it's honest." She cocked her head at him. "Do you want to know what I said back there, at the station?"

"I'm all ears."

I reached for her. "Eve, no."

"I said you were a filthy bloodsucker lover. And you've just confirmed it, General. Turning your back on your own kind, blathering on about the finer points of our benevolent prince, trying to trick us into feeling at ease enough to talk to you." She smiled at him, but her face glowed with hate. "But I don't need to be tricked into telling the truth, so here it is. I hope you get what's coming to you. I hope they drain you dry when they're done with you."

"Ah, I see." The general leaned back, all pretenses of friendliness vanished. "A rebel. In cheap shoes, from a bad neighborhood, no less."

"I'm not afraid of you." Eve's eyes blazed. "Some of us don't have anything left to lose."

The general smiled, but the friendly grandfather was nowhere to be found. Instead, his smile was ice, making my blood run cold. "In the end, there's one thing we *all* have to lose. You'd best remember that."

"What's that?" Eve scoffed.

He leaned forward, the late-afternoon sun glinting off the thin film of snot collected on his mustache.

"Your soul."

CHAPTER 5
GULP

I GRIPPED EVE'S ARM THE REST OF THE RIDE, PRAYING SHE'D KEEP silent. I tried not to think about what the general had said. He ignored us, watching the palace as it came into view.

It was grand, and as he'd said, even more beautiful than in the propaganda videos. Expansive grounds led up to the castle. An enormous fountain bubbled in front of the curved flagstone drive.

It was the largest and most beautiful building I'd ever seen.

The manor was pale-gray stone, its peaks rising high into the sky. The setting sun cast a pinkish hue over the edifice, making it look as though it glowed magically from within. The roof was etched with copper that had long since oxidized, its aqua patina luminescent in the dying light. I counted twelve chimneys. *Twelve.*

Even Eve gaped as the carriage brought us closer. The general gave her a quick glance. "I'm sure the castle won't impress the likes of you."

"I'm speechless, for once," Eve admitted.

The carriage rolled to a stop, and a butler opened the door, helping us down the steps. My knees wobbled as I looked up at the grand palace. A dozen servants came through the front doors. They lined up, prim and proper in their pressed black-and-white uniforms. I moved closer to Eve as we waited for the other carriages to arrive. The general started talking to one of the staff, and I tugged Eve's hand urgently.

"You need to tone it down. What you said wasn't safe, and it wasn't smart."

Her chin jutted out. "I'm not trying to play it safe, and I certainly wasn't trying to impress anyone. I told him what I thought. What I *think*."

"Keep your voice down and your opinions to yourself." I eyed the servants. "We're sort of surrounded."

"I'm not afraid."

I sighed. "Well, that makes one of us. Please keep your mouth shut for me, or at least, so you live long enough to eat another sandwich."

Eve rolled her eyes, but at least she smiled a little. She motioned to the palace. "I heard this place was built back in the old America."

"Who lived here?" My family had been wealthy, but the idea of someone living in this uber-mansion was baffling.

She stared at the building. "Some rich guy. But he died, and then his wife married someone else. I think they turned it into a hotel or something before the war."

"How do you know all of this?" One thing we didn't study at the academy was history. It was considered too controversial.

She shrugged. "One good thing about the slum school was that it was in an old, crumbling building that used to be the city library. I stole every book I found."

"History books?" I was shocked. I'd thought they'd all gone the way of the cell phone.

"You don't get out much, do you?"

I furrowed my brow. *Raised in a bubble, indeed.*

The other carriages arrived, and activity bustled around us. Butlers opened carriage doors, and the other contestants filed out. The staff watched as the girls gaped at the building. The general went to the top step and cleared his throat. "Ladies, please form a line. The royal family will receive you inside."

I sucked in a deep breath and got into line behind Eve. We climbed the stairs, the servants nodding politely as we passed.

Eve turned and took one last look at the grounds. "It's been nice knowing you," she joked.

I couldn't respond. My nerves thrummed, and my palms sweated as we crossed the threshold into the lobby. In spite of our orders to keep our mouths shut, all the girls murmured in wonder as we entered the palace.

The enormous foyer was a pale marble, with a soaring ceiling and a winding, grand staircase in the center of the room. A chandelier lit with hundreds of candles glowed from above. Enormous windows lined the sweeping stairs. The room glowed as the sun finalized its transit and dipped below the horizon, fiery pinks and oranges lighting its descent and reflecting off the marble.

The general motioned to the stairs, and we all fell silent. Just as the sun disappeared completely, we heard footsteps echoing down the staircase.

My mouth went dry as I waited. Three armed sentinels descended first. They wore the purples, reds, and deep blues that marked them as members of the royal family guard. The guards' skin was pale, the whitest ivory. I shivered as they took their places next to the general. They were so pale compared to him that they looked positively ghoulish.

The general spoke to the guards in low tones, his gaze flicking intermittently to Eve. I had the urge to hide her behind me, but she stood firm, shoulders squared, jaw taut.

More footsteps thundered on the grand staircase.

I saw his boots first—tall, black, polished to a reflective brilliance. His powerfully muscled legs came next, then his broad chest adorned in a black ceremonial uniform replete with a deep-purple sash. Then the prince's handsome face came into view. He had a square jaw, patrician nose, and broad cheekbones. His thick, dark-brown hair was tousled, and his deep-brown eyes radiated intelligence and...was it kindness? He was tall and handsome, all right. He was also pale, with a white patina to his skin that made him look unearthly.

One of the guards cleared his throat. "His Royal Highness, Prince Dallas Black, Crown Prince of The United Settlements."

He made it to the landing, nodded at us, and smiled, flashing a deep dimple on his left cheek.

I thought I heard some of the girls sigh.

He looked pleased, as if he expected the response. "Good evening." His voice was deep and rich. "Thank you so much for accepting our invitation to the Pageant. We're so pleased to welcome you to the palace." Another winning smile.

Eve shot me a brief look, as if to say, "Like we had a choice." But even she couldn't keep from staring at the handsome, strange prince.

More footsteps sounded, and the king and queen descended the stairs next.

The same guard announced them. "His Royal Majesty, King Reginald Black, Crown King of the United Royal Settlements. Her Royal Majesty, Queen Serena Black, Crown Queen of the United Royal Settlements."

King Black was tall and muscular, handsome like his son. He had gray hair and a trim, white beard. But it was the queen who drew my gaze and held it. The propaganda films hadn't done her justice. Her beauty was striking. She was tall and lean, with sapphire-blue eyes, a high forehead, and a long, elegant neck. Her platinum hair was surprisingly loose, waving down past the shoulders of her cerulean-blue brocade dress. I couldn't tell how old she was. Her smooth, alabaster skin showed no lines.

Both she and the king inclined their heads to one of the guards as he whispered to them. It was the same guard who'd spoken to the general. Icicles jabbed down my spine. Would he tell them about Eve's brazen words?

The king cleared his throat and nodded at us. Unlike the prince, who exuded easy, casual charm, his movements were stiff and uncomfortable. "Thank you for joining us in our home. In a few moments, the general will take you to one of our conference rooms, where you'll be briefed by the royal emissary. I'm sure you're tired from a long day of travel. You'll be taken to your chambers shortly and served dinner there. The rest of the contestants will be joining us later this evening. Preparation for the Pageant will begin tomorrow morning promptly after breakfast."

The queen cleared her throat and took a step forward. "I'd like to say a few words." She smiled at us without warmth, and the prince's brow furrowed as he watched her. "You are very welcome in our home. But I might remind you that this *is* our home, and you will respect us while you remain here."

The girls looked at each other nervously, and Eve's throat worked as she swallowed.

"Now, do any of you feel as though you won't be able to maintain a modicum of decorum while a guest in the palace? If so, it would be best to address it now before you get settled."

The prince tensed and looked at his father, his eyebrows raised in a silent question. The king only shook his head.

No one said a word, but Eve took a step forward. "Me." Her voice was hoarse.

My heart sank.

"Is that so? And what, may I ask, is your name?" The queen also stepped forward, her pale skin glowing in the darkening room.

"Eve. Eve Whitely, Settlement Four." She straightened her spine.

"The general mentioned you had some concerns." The queen came closer, her heels clicking against the marble tiles. "What do you have to say about it?"

Eve stood her ground. "I was chosen for this competition, but I'm not the sort of girl you're looking for."

The queen arched an eyebrow. "And what sort of girl is that?"

Eve crossed her arms over her chest. "The kind that will tolerate a proposal from a filthy bloodsucker like the prince. The kind that will stay here and jump through your hoops."

A collective gasp filled the room. My eyes filled with tears. *Eve, no.*

"Ah." Now the queen's smile met her eyes. "So you think me and my family *filthy*."

The muscle in Eve's jaw jumped. "That's what I said."

In a flash of cerulean, the queen appeared next to Eve. She grabbed her by the hair and dragged her into the middle of the room.

Eve screamed, then the other girls joined in. The prince shot to his feet, but his father held his hand out, ordering him to stop.

"Eve!" But her name died on my lips as the queen wrenched Eve's head to the side, exposing her neck.

"Silence!" the queen ordered.

The guards surrounded us on both sides, protecting the queen in the center of the room and closing off the exits.

Eve's wild gaze found mine. "No. *No!*" She struggled, but

the queen held her firm, her grip unnaturally strong. "Let me go!"

"I don't think so. We'll see what you have to say after *this*." The queen leaned back and opened her mouth. Two long, sharp fangs glittered in the candlelight.

Oh my God, it's true.

Oh my God, No!

She plunged her fangs into Eve's neck.

Eve fought in vain, her shrieks echoing across the marble as the queen drank deeply. I heard the girl next to me sobbing.

Frozen, I watched in horror as the queen finished feeding and dropped Eve to the ground. My new friend's aqua eyes were wide with shock. A trickle of blood dripped down her neck.

I couldn't tell if she was alive or dead.

The queen straightened herself. She wiped the blood from the corner of her mouth, then cleaned her hand off on her dress, bright crimson against azure.

The royal guard came and dragged Eve away.

"Now," said the queen, turning to face us, "does anyone else have an objection?"

No one said a word.

The prince stormed from the room, following the sentinels who had Eve.

And I just stood there, shaking.

CHAPTER 6
STILL SHAKING

NONE OF US DARED TO SPEAK AS WE FOLLOWED THE GENERAL OUT of the foyer. *You will obey me.* I'd wildly underestimated the weight of that threat.

I wanted to cry—and scream—but I was too afraid. Shocked by what had happened, I had no idea what to expect or what to do next. *Where is Eve?* Had the queen killed her so quickly? No life had glittered in Eve's aqua eyes, but had she been in shock?

What happens when a vampire drinks your blood?

I had no desire to find out. I just hoped there was a chance my friend had survived.

So it was true. The royal family were vampires. The winner of this contest would marry a vampire.

WTF?

"Ladies," the general said, "follow me."

I shivered as we followed him, lambs to the slaughter. We turned a corner and entered what looked like a large, fancy parlor. "Sit down." The general motioned to the chairs and couches dotted throughout the room. He paced back and forth in front of a roaring fire. I barely noticed the details of the luxurious rugs, tapestries, and furniture surrounding me as I sank down into a chair, its back to the wall.

I didn't want anyone to sneak up on me.

"I'm sorry you all had to witness that." The kindly version of the general was back, his face lit with sympathy. "But the royal family will not tolerate disrespect in their own home. And they shouldn't have to."

I'd never seen so many girls so silent. No one seemed to breathe.

"I told the young lady earlier that the rules are to be obeyed. Let Eve from Settlement Four be a lesson to you all. You will speak when spoken to, and you will always be polite to the royal family and the entire staff. Any insurrection will not be tolerated. Is that understood?"

Everyone, myself included, murmured their assent.

"Good. The royal emissary will be here in a moment to explain more about the Pageant. The training begins promptly tomorrow morning, and the competition itself begins next week. For now, I want to leave you with a few simple rules. First of all, not a word of what just happened is allowed outside of the palace. If anyone is caught disseminating this information, it will be considered high treason. The guilty party will be sentenced to death."

We gaped at him and at each other. I put a hand over my rioting heart, willing it to calm down.

He paced some more while he continued. "Now, on to the more mundane details. You are to attend every class and training that is scheduled. There are no exceptions. If you are too ill to attend a session, your maids must notify the royal emissary, and you will be screened by the palace physician. Breakfast, lunch, and dinner will all be served in the common room, located off the kitchen. You must be present at all meals. You will return to your room each night before the sun sets, and you will not leave until the following morning when the sun has risen. Does everyone understand?"

"Yes, sir."

"During the day, when you aren't at lessons, you are allowed outside in the gardens and on the grounds, as permitted by the royal emissary. Your personal guards must be notified of your whereabouts at all times. You are allowed to write home once per week, but please be advised that all correspondence to and from the palace is screened for security purposes. Any questions?"

I had nothing but questions, but I kept my mouth firmly shut.

The doors opened, and sentinels lined the entrance. A tall, lithe young man with slicked-back black hair strode in, dressed in a deep-purple ceremonial uniform, a cape trailing behind him. He stepped to the front of the room, dismissing the general with a nod.

The general swept from the room. I was relieved to see him go.

"Ladies. I trust you've had an eventful afternoon." The man's dark eyes sparkled in the firelight. *Was he joking?*

"I'm Tariq, the royal emissary and the master of ceremonies for the Pageant. I was very involved with the selection of each contestant." He cleared his throat, then smirked. "Obviously, my choices weren't flawless."

My jaw dropped.

"I know the general mentioned that discretion about this matter is of the utmost importance. No one is allowed to speak about what happened here this evening—not to your families, not the press, not to your best friend. Any violation of this order will result in your immediate dismissal from the contest, your arrest, and shortly thereafter, your execution."

One of the girls in the front row clutched her stomach.

Tariq arched an eyebrow at her. "Get ahold of yourself, young lady. This is the big leagues. They require appropriate big-girl panties."

I briefly looked at the girl next to me to see if she was as appalled as I was, but she stared straight ahead, her fists clenched in her lap.

Tariq stalked prettily at the front of the room and continued. "I have high hopes that you and the contestants from the western settlements, who'll join us later, will all fare well. I will oversee every aspect of the contest, including your branding, grooming, and preparation."

He motioned to the sentinels, and they left the room, closing the door behind them. "And now, I'd like you all to relax. You're safe here with me, and I can promise there won't be another unscripted outburst like the one you just witnessed."

He walked closer, weaving in and out of our seats, pausing to examine each girl. He clucked his approval or tsked with distaste then moved on to the next one. When he got to me, he picked up a braid and eyed it. "Nicely done. And I approve of your traveling dress. Gwyneth, correct? Settlement Four?"

"Yes. And thank you," I said, trying to mind my manners. I smoothed my dress. "My mother picked out my dress."

Up close, I could see that his eyelashes fanned out and curved seductively and his lips were full and sensuous. His dark hair was combed back stylishly, and he smelled of cologne, foreign and expensive.

In the dim light of the room, Tariq looked human. But was he?

"No doubt. I remember your mother from your file. She's a stunner." He continued working his ways through the girls until he came back to the front of the room. "Now, let's get down to business, shall we? In this session, you are allowed to speak freely and ask questions *when I tell you*. However, I don't recommend *ever* maligning the royal family while you're here at the palace. Your little friend back there is proof of what can happen. Are we clear?"

"Yes, sir."

"All right." He put his hands on his hips. "Who has a question?"

Everyone started shouting at once.

"Did the queen kill her?"

"Are they going to eat us?"

"How am I supposed to focus on anything other than watching out for my neck?"

"Was that real?"

"Can I go home?"

"Do we have roommates?"

"Is it considered high treason if we talk about what happened amongst ourselves?"

"How long does the contest last?"

"What sort of clothes will we wear? Can we pick them out?"

"Will I have my own stylist?"

"Is there a gym somewhere?"

Tariq, clearly taken aback by the onslaught, held up his hands. "Whoa, whoa. Silence!"

Everyone stopped talking at once.

Tariq ran a hand through his hair. "I'd forgotten what girls are like. The questions, the hormones. Now, collect yourselves, and raise your hands. I'll call on you one at a time."

Almost all the girls immediately raised their hands, and he called on one near the front. She wore a pink sari, and her dark, wavy hair hung halfway down her back. "I'm not maligning the royal family, but I have to ask—was that real? Is the queen…" She let the question trail off, too afraid to speak the words aloud.

Tariq nodded. He understood exactly where she was headed. "The queen, the entire royal family, and many of the sentinels here at the palace are different from ordinary humans. Where you and I are ordinary, they are…*extra*ordinary, in the very literal sense of the word."

So the royal emissary was human, after all.

The girl in the sari raised her hand again, and Tariq nodded at her. "And that means what, exactly?"

"It means they have powers we don't have, they have different needs, and they are stronger than us. Much stronger."

I raised my hand. "Is Eve still alive?"

Tariq's gaze met mine. "I don't know. But don't ask about her again. The whole palace is in an uproar about what she said." He turned and looked each of the other girls in the eyes. "The royal family is staging the Pageant to heal the rift between the monarchy and the settlements. They want to unite us all and bring the settlements into the future stronger. That's why you're here. It's something for the settlers to get excited about—a princess of their own, a princess of the people. But hate speech and prejudice of any kind won't be tolerated here, just like it's not tolerated in the settlements. The Northerners conquered us, and they were generous enough to let us live. Now, the royal family's generosity has extended to this contest, in the hopes that they can bring peace and prosperity to the settlements."

More girls anxiously raised their hands, but the door burst open. The prince strode through, flanked by two armed guards. "Tariq, I'm sorry to interrupt, but may I address the contestants?"

"Of course, Your Highness." Tariq swept into a deep bow.

When he rose, he motioned for us to rise and imitate him. We all mimicked Tariq as he dipped into a curtsy.

"Thank you." The prince nodded. Tariq left the room quickly, his sentinels following closely behind.

Prince Black turned toward us. If possible, his face had gotten even paler.

"I'm so sorry for what my mother did." His gaze sought out each of ours. "She's—my mother, I mean—she's very old school. She's proud, and she has a lot of rigid ideas about respect and honor. In her time, no human would dare speak to a...queen...that way. The king and I have spoken to her, and she's very sorry to have frightened you all. She understands what she did wasn't, er, very welcoming." His hands clenched at his sides. "I can assure you nothing like that will happen again during your time here. You have my word."

He nodded at us stiffly, clearly embarrassed. "Well, good night. Tariq will be back to see you to your rooms." He left without another word, and Tariq came in immediately.

Still shaking, I followed the royal emissary to my room.

CHAPTER 7
TURNED

MY BEDROOM WAS FIT FOR A PRINCESS. THE CEILINGS SOARED. I could see the stars coming out in the darkening night sky through the floor-to-ceiling windows. Lush gold brocade drapes elegantly outlined the view.

There was a full-length gilded mirror and an elegant chandelier. A fire was roaring in the fireplace, and the large four-poster bed looked luxurious and warm with its gold-and-black velvet comforter.

But I couldn't get excited about my new room. All I could think of was Eve and how the queen had ravaged her.

I sank down onto my bed. What the hell had I gotten myself into?

There was a knock on the door, and I jumped. A pretty young woman in uniform opened the door. "We're your staff," she said in a friendly tone. "Can we come in and introduce ourselves?"

"Of course."

I stood as three maids entered. The one who'd spoken was also the tallest, fair and blonde. She was followed by two younger maids who had to be identical twins. The twins had coffee-colored skin and almond-shaped eyes.

The three of them curtsied before me.

"I'm Gwyneth West, Settlement Four." I smiled at them. "And you never need to curtsy to me again, although I appreciate the gesture."

"Yes, miss. I'm Evangeline, your head maid." The tallest girl nodded. "This is Bria and Bettina, who are also in your service."

"Our pleasure, miss," they said. They smiled so similarly that it spooked me.

"For the record, I'm Bettina. I always wear a pink ribbon in my hair." Bettina pulled her braid forward so I could see the marker.

"And I'm Bria. I wear a blue ribbon." Her sister showed me hers.

"Forgive me if I confuse you at first. I'll get the hang of it eventually."

"Yes, miss." They spoke in unison, which was very unnerving.

Evangeline stepped forward. "It's our job to keep your room clean, help prepare you each morning for your lessons, and help you dress for special events." Her eyes sparkled.

"Special events?" Tariq hadn't mentioned any special events. He'd been too busy trying to convince us we weren't all going to die.

"Yes, miss. For the balls and any special dates with the prince."

My stomach twisted at the thought of being alone with one of the royals. "Oh."

"Miss, if I may…?" Evangeline started.

"Please speak freely."

She pointed to herself and to the twins. "We're human too.

And we've never had any trouble with the royal family. Isn't that right, girls?"

The twins nodded earnestly, and Evangeline continued. "There was one kitchen cook who had a problem with the royal family's…er, *heritage*, and she said something nasty once, right in front of the king. He fired her on the spot and sent her packing. But he didn't touch her. He wouldn't do something like that. Neither would the prince. But the queen is different. She's very old—you'd never know it by looking at her—and she's very proper. I mean to say, she's *Northern* proper. She's still not used to our ways."

I arched an eyebrow. "So she occasionally eats rude humans?"

"No, not at all, miss." Evangeline shook her head vehemently. "She's never hurt one of the staff, and there are several hundred of us here. But we've been through sensitivity training, and we know not to speak like…like that young lady did."

Sensitivity training so they don't insult the vampires. Now I've heard everything.

I dug my nails into my palms. "That young lady was my friend, and she was expressing her opinion. Not something she should've been killed for."

Evangeline's eyes were wide. "No, miss. Of course not. And I'm so sorry about it. My point is that the queen had never heard words like that spoken under this roof. I don't think she could control herself. Where she comes from, it was so disrespectful that she *had* to act to save her family's honor."

I sank down onto the bed. "Is that supposed to make me feel better?"

Evangeline came closer. "I was hoping it would, but I can see I'm only making things worse. My point is that I've been here for two years, and I've never seen anything like what happened tonight."

"They mostly leave us alone," Bettina offered. "We work during daylight hours, and when the sun's down, we go straight to our rooms unless there's an event. But none of us have ever had any trouble that I know of."

"Does the queen have human maids?"

Bria shook her head. "She brought her own maids from the North, which I think means she's pretty self-aware."

I couldn't help it—I laughed. "Well, that's good, I guess. Do you know anything about their…feeding habits?" I'd begun wondering if they kept a supply of humans in the pantry.

All three maids shook their heads. "They don't eat human food. But they drink wine."

"But you keep a full kitchen staff?"

They nodded. "They feed us very well. That's why most of us took the jobs. Most of the staff came from Settlement Eight." Settlement Eight was notoriously poor, with perpetual freezing weather and crops that refused to grow.

"We came here out of desperation," Evangeline admitted. "But they've treated us incredibly well. I swear it."

I nodded. Either these girls were brainwashed, or the royal family didn't regularly dine on civilians.

There was another knock on the door, and Evangeline furrowed her brow. "Yes? Who is it?"

"The prince."

The girls looked at each other, shocked. "Yes, Your Highness! Just a minute!" They flew about the already immaculate room, fluffing pillows, straightening chairs, and stoking the fire. Bettina quickly fixed my hair and pinched my cheeks so they'd have color.

"Ow!"

She winked at me, then all three of them stood to the side as the prince swept in with two of his guards.

I stood and curtsied. "Your Highness."

He bowed, rising slowly, forcing me to confront his broad, handsome face and square jaw. The firelight bathed him in gold tones, making it look as if he was lit from within, a golden, smoldering god. "Miss West. I've come with news of your friend."

"Please." I motioned for him to sit down, my heart thudding.

He sank into the closest chair, looking too large for it. "I'm so sorry about what my mother did. She's mortified, if it makes you feel any better."

"It doesn't." The sharp words were out of my mouth before I could retrieve them.

He sighed, his face puckering into a frown. "I'm not surprised. Her actions were unforgivable."

He sounded sincere, but the last thing I was going to do was let my guard down. "You said you had news?"

"Eve is in the medical ward."

"She's alive?"

He nodded, but his jaw was taut. He flexed his fingers then clenched his hands into fists.

"Is she going to make it?"

"She will…live. But she won't be as she was before."

I shook my head, not understanding. "What does that mean?"

"It means my mother drank too much of Eve's blood. Your friend did not survive her human life."

I looked to my maids, but they stared straight ahead.

"You said she would live—"

"But not as a human," the prince interrupted gently. "She won't be the same."

I pulled at the collar of my dress. The room was suddenly stifling hot. "I don't understand."

His dark gaze met mine. "She's been turned."

His words did not compute. "Turned, like you turn a roast in the oven?"

Evangeline looked at me funny but quickly turned away.

The prince winced. "No. Turned as in turned into something else. Are you okay, Miss West? You look pale."

"Turned into *what*?" I hiss-whispered, even though I didn't want to know the answer.

Even though I already knew the answer.

He raked a hand through his hair, making it spiky and a little wild. "Turned into one of my kind. Vampire."

"Please take that back." The floor seemed to tilt beneath my feet. "Eve doesn't want to be a filthy bloodsucker."

My maids gasped.

I was vaguely worried he would drain me dry for my treacherous words, but he didn't move from his seat.

"No offense, Your Highness." The apology came out thickly, as if I were underwater.

"I understand this wouldn't have been your friend's choice." The prince sighed. "And I appreciate you've had a terrible shock."

I remembered the look of terror in Eve's eyes as the queen sank her fangs into her neck. "Terrible—yes, that's the word." I took a wobbly step backward, as if I could escape the conversation. The room spun around me.

"Miss West?" The prince shot to his feet.

The last thing I saw as I hit the floor was his shiny boots, polished to a lustrous, depthless black.

I WOKE TO EVANGELINE PRESSING A COLD CLOTH TO MY FOREHEAD.

"Are you all right, miss?"

"What time is it?" I was disoriented, my voice raspy.

"Almost midnight."

I nodded. "Sorry about that. About fainting." I'd never fainted in my life. "And what I said to the prince." I peeked at her.

"His Highness understood. You had a great shock." She shushed me and shook her head. "To be honest, we were all surprised."

I sat up a little. "Why were you surprised?"

Her eyes were wide as she handed me a glass of water. "I didn't know what happened when they bit a human. I didn't know they could change us."

I took a shaky sip. "It's not exactly good news."

"No." Evangeline got busy folding cloths, arranging them neatly on the bedside table. "Still, it was kind that the prince came here to talk to you. He seemed very upset about what his mother did."

"It's not exactly a great way to start the competition." I watched her continue to fold, wondering how much I could get away with asking her. "Do you know what will happen to Eve?"

"No, miss. The staff's been talking about it all night, of course. But the nurse on call only said the girl's got a fever, and she's tossing and turning. There's nothing they can do for her except watch. I heard the queen sent some Northerners to the medical ward to attend her, but that's all I know."

I nodded. "And the prince? What happened with him after I…collapsed?"

Evangeline took my glass and carefully set it down. "He stayed until the doctor checked on you. He picked you up and put you on the bed himself."

I cringed, imagining him carrying my inert body. The image was beyond awkward, especially because of the way I'd insulted him. *Filthy bloodsucker.*

"He was very gentle."

I nodded, unwilling to say more. Evangeline seemed completely loyal to the royals, in spite of what they'd done.

She eyed me. "I only say that because you seem afraid of him."

I sat up further. "I *am* afraid of him. Aren't you?"

Evangeline shook her head. "No, miss. Like I said, I've never been mistreated here. The others say the same thing. We've never been afraid. But with all the girls here, all the excitement about the contest, it might just be a lot for them to handle, especially the queen. She's been quite isolated."

"You're making excuses for her?"

Evangeline smoothed the comforter. "It's just that respect is very important to them. That was the first thing we learned in training. They take words seriously. They aren't ashamed of being what they are, but they won't tolerate cruelty and prejudice in others."

"Maybe they should have put a warning in the invite. Except it wasn't an invite—it was an order. And Eve didn't want to be here, but she followed the law."

She nodded. "The emissary's search committee should have known about her politics. She should never have been brought to the palace."

I pulled my comforter up. "But she was, and look where it got her."

The maid patted my hand. "You should rest. Tomorrow's a long day. The twins and I will be in bright and early with your new wardrobe. We'll need to do your hair and makeup, all the bells and whistles."

I nodded. But as soon as she closed the door, I hopped out of bed.

With all that had transpired, bells and whistles were the least of my concerns.

CHAPTER 8
IN THE MIDNIGHT HOUR

I TOOK A DEEP, SHAKY BREATH THEN OPENED THE DOOR. THE hallway was dimly lit, and my guard was nowhere to be seen.

I crept quietly toward the stairs. I didn't know where the medical wing was, but I remembered the direction in which they'd dragged Eve.

I had to find her. I had to make sure she was okay.

The general said we weren't allowed out of our rooms after the sun had set. I didn't let myself think about why as I stole down the stairs.

The grand foyer was empty. I could hear music and voices drifting from one of the rooms nearby, but I saw no one. No sentinels guarded the entryway. Was that because they were human? Were they, too, banned from roaming the castle after hours?

I headed in the direction I'd seen Eve being taken. The palace was dark, only dim lanterns lighting the cavernous hall. I shivered and wrapped my arms around myself, half wishing I was back upstairs under my velvet comforter, my fire keeping me warm. But my mother's words echoed inside my head.

You're a West, and that means you don't give up, and you don't get to roll over and hide your eyes.

I'd seen what the queen had done to Eve. But my friend, however reckless, hadn't deserved her fate. Eve needed to know she still had an ally, to know she wasn't alone in this strange and terrible place.

Still, I'd promised my mother. *For the love of all things holy, stay alive.* I had to be careful.

I stayed close to the wall and kept moving forward. There was light ahead and voices. I wondered if I'd found the medical ward. As I drew closer, I could hear the conversation more distinctly.

"Have you seen this happen before?" a woman asked.

"Not like this. It's the fastest transformation I've witnessed," another woman answered. "We need to be prepared for her to wake up sooner than we planned."

"We have plenty of supplies from the bank. We should be fine."

The other woman tsked. "It's a pity. She's very young."

"She made her own bed."

I crept closer, hoping to catch a glimpse of Eve.

"Miss West," a deep, smooth voice said suddenly from behind me, "aren't you out awfully late?"

I whirled, my heart stuttering.

The prince stepped out of the shadows. He arched an eyebrow as he looked me from head to toe. "It's nice to see you conscious, my lady, but I'm afraid you're in violation of curfew."

"Um. I… I, um…"

He smiled a little, more amused than scolding, and my shoulders relaxed. But then footsteps thundered toward us, and the prince's face turned stormy. "Don't say a word, and don't move." He grabbed my hand and pulled me behind his back so that I was covered by his cape, pressed up against his body. I held my breath, but not before I got a heady whiff of his scent, masculine and earthy.

Do all vampires smell this good?

The footsteps came closer. My heart thudded so loudly that I feared they'd be able to hear it.

"Your Highness." A sentinel stopped in front of us.

"What is all the ruckus about?" The prince sounded pissed, and quite frankly, a little scary.

"One of the ladies is missing from her room."

"Which one?" the prince asked.

"The other girl from Settlement Four."

"I'll take care of it. Send the others back to their posts. Have you spoken with the king or queen?" I felt his big body tense.

"No, Your Highness. We wanted to handle it first."

"Don't say a word to them. That's an order. After the debacle earlier this evening, I think we should spare my parents any more worries. I will handle the girl. Understood?"

"Of course, Your Highness. I'll tell the others, and we'll return to our posts immediately."

The prince waited until they were gone, then he lifted his cape and let me out from under it. "Sorry about that," he said. "Not a very dignified hiding place."

"Don't apologize." I shook my head. "You just saved me."

Even as shadows played across his face, it softened. "You were attempting to see your friend, I presume?"

I nodded.

"You shouldn't." He took in my rumpled traveling dress and sleep-mussed hair. "She's not in any shape for visitors, and you don't appear to be, either. Let's get you to your room before my mother finds you and declares you dessert, shall we?"

I shivered. "Y-yes."

Seeing the look of absolute horror on my face, he frowned. "That was a joke."

"Oh," I said, shakily. "Ha-ha."

Brow furrowed, he muttered something under his breath and took me by the elbow. "If we see anyone else, don't say a word."

I nodded. I was probably too petrified to speak, anyway.

We swept down the hall. Now the sentinels manned their posts at regular intervals. They pretended not to see us, looking straight ahead. Each of them was pale, their skin almost silver in the darkness.

Sensing my distraction, the prince nodded toward one of them. "At night, we only have the Black Guard. During the day, human guards protect the palace."

With rumblings of a revolt on the horizon, the all-human guard seemed…ill-advised. I didn't say anything for a moment until we were up the stairs and out of earshot. "You trust them?"

This was *so* not my business. Still, my genuine curiosity about this new world and the intersection of our kinds got the better of me.

The prince looked at me sharply. "Who?"

"Your human guards?"

"With my life, my lady." We reached my door, and he bowed formally. I fumbled through my curtsy and caught a flash of it again—his dimple. "There's a lot you don't know about my family and about our kind. We've existed peacefully with our staff and our human guards since we came here. If you ask them, I believe they'll tell you we treat them fairly and they aren't afraid. They're happy to be here."

My maids seemed thrilled with the arrangement. But as they'd come from the frozen, starving tundra known as Settlement 8, what else were they going to say?

The prince tilted his chin, inspecting me. "I've brought you and the others here because I'm invested in this competition. It's important to me. I want our kinds to rule the land together, human and vampire."

He mentioned nothing of love, nothing of finding someone to share his life with. Any far-off inkling I'd had of this being a search to find the prince's soulmate vanished. "So this competition is strictly for politics?"

He bristled. "Don't say it like it's a bad thing. The safety and prosperity of the settlements are of the utmost importance. In addition, I fully expect to make a match for love. That's the only way the union could last. I must be able to trust that my wife is committed to both my family and me."

I thought of the other girls sobbing as his mother ravaged Eve's neck. *Good luck with that.* But then I looked at the prince's handsome face. Even with such odds, he would probably manage just fine.

"I have high hopes for the Pageant." He crossed his powerful arms over his chest. "I want to bring peace to the settlements, and our races to live together in harmony. That's the only way we'll all survive."

"Survive? Survive what, exactly?"

His eyes flashed. "Threats to the settlements."

"What threats?"

He took a step back. "It's late, my lady. You need to rest. But before I let you go, I need you to promise me something."

I waited for him to go on.

"No one can know you were out of your room tonight. I don't want you to be made an example of."

"I promise." I couldn't get the words out fast enough. I had *zero* desire to be another case study.

"Then I take my leave."

"Wait—*wait*. What will happen with Eve?"

The prince blew out a deep breath. "Her new life will begin soon. Is it enough that I promise to bring you news?"

No, I thought.

"Yes," I said.

"I will meet with you tomorrow and answer questions about your friend." He bowed again. "Until then."

It wasn't good enough, but at least it was something. "Until then." I nodded instead of fumbling through another curtsy.

The prince's cape sailed out behind him as he strode away without giving me a backward glance.

CHAPTER 9
IT'S COMPLICATED

I WOKE TO MY MAIDS FUSSING AROUND THE ROOM AND SQUEALING over each new dress they hung in my closet.

"Can you *believe* what the seamstresses came up with?" Bettina gushed "Everything's so gorgeous!"

Bria's eyes shone. "Now we know what they've been working on for all these months."

Evangeline beamed as she held up a golden-hued frock. "This is fit for a princess. I cannot wait to see Miss West in this!"

I groaned and pulled my covers up, watching them bustle. In the light of day, my situation seemed dire.

My only friend at the palace was in the medical wing, becoming a vampire because she'd insulted the royal family and my hostess, the queen, had bitten her. *The vampire queen.*

Speaking of vampires, I was surrounded by them and the humans who loyally protected them against threats.

Speaking of threats, apparently, the settlements were in danger. The prince had said as much. He said the royals and the settlers needed to work together to survive.

Speaking of the prince—the vampire prince—he'd

admitted that the Pageant was for political purposes but that he also wanted to fall in love with the winner.

I'd come here to win. But we hadn't even started, and I was already screwed.

There was no way the prince would fall in love with me. Not now. My first night at the palace, and I'd already passed out in front of him, broken explicit rules, and insulted his family terribly.

But the fact that I wasn't exactly princess material wasn't my only problem.

I was afraid. Afraid of the Dark Prince, afraid of his family, afraid of his world.

You promised Mom. You promised to try.

The prince seemed kind, the prince was handsome, and the prince was tall and strapping. He was also a vampire. A vampire like his mother, the queen, who'd just ravaged my friend.

A vampire, like the ones my father and brother had gone off to fight, never to return.

Rage bloomed in my chest, but I pushed it aside. I pictured Winnie and Remy asleep next to the fire, huddled together for warmth. They were innocent.

They were also my responsibility.

I didn't get to be a coward. I would try to win the prince's heart because it was the only way to save my family. If I didn't do something, the West clan would be begging in the streets by summer. I owed my family my best effort, even if trying to make the vampire prince fall in love with me and propose was already utterly hopeless.

Even if my own heart thundered in a mixture of terror and fury at the thought.

"MY LADY, YOU ARE STUNNING." EVANGELINE FINISHED TYING the back and adjusted the emerald velvet of my gown.

The twins put the final touches on my hair and makeup then stepped back. "Wow," Bria said.

"Just gorgeous," agreed Bettina.

"Have a look." Evangeline encouraged me toward the full-length mirror.

I sucked in a deep breath when I saw my reflection. My hair flowed in loose waves around my shoulders. My face shimmered with just the right amount of makeup. I looked healthy and slightly sparkly, but not over-done. Large tear-drop emerald earrings glinted against my pale skin. The velvet of the dark-green dress, the same hue as the jewels I wore, glowed in the early morning sunlight. The brocade front fit snugly, accentuating my curves.

"It's lovely. Thank you."

Evangeline shook her head. "The dress is pretty, but *you* steal the show. I think the prince will approve."

I blew out a shuddery breath. "We'll see."

There was a knock on the door. "Come in," Evangeline instructed.

Tariq poked his head through, his shellacked hair reflecting the sunlight. "Ah, Gwyneth. You're looking lovely."

I curtsied. "Good morning, Tariq."

He held out his hand for me. Did I imagine it, or did Evangeline and the twins give him disapproving looks? I didn't have time to ask. I took his hand, and he swept me from the room without giving me a chance to say goodbye. He hustled me down the hall.

"Where are we going?"

"I need to speak with you. Privately."

He threw open the door to a small study and ushered me

inside. He closed the door then whirled on me, cape flying. "Where were you last night?"

"In my room." *Until I snuck out.*

"I have verified information that you were out of your room in the middle of the night, in direct violation of curfew." A vein throbbed in his temple. "What do you have to say to that?"

"I have—"

The door burst open, and the prince stormed in. He wore a dark-gray tunic, and his hair was a bit wild, as if he'd run to cut us off. "She has nothing to say, Tariq."

I watched, shocked, as the prince slammed the door behind him. He glowered at Tariq. "Miss West was with me last night. We were getting to know each other better."

"Of course." Tariq shrugged, immediately feigning indifference, as if he hadn't been about to pop a blood vessel moments earlier. "I was just checking in with the lady, Your Highness. I'm in charge of the contestants. They're my responsibility. I can't have them out at all hours, running about. Especially after what already happened."

"The contestants are ultimately *my* responsibility." The prince took a step toward him. "I don't want you harassing the girls, Tariq. We both know you get a little grabby when there's power lying about."

The emissary's eyes flashed. "My lord, I wasn't—"

"I do not approve of the tone you were using with Miss West, nor do I approve of you dragging her away from her maids and into this room. It's our responsibility to keep these young women safe, and I don't want them to feel vulnerable or scared while they're here at the palace. Yesterday was bad enough."

Tariq nodded, any trace of dissent vanished from his handsome, now-compliant face. "Of course, my lord. You're right."

"And as for having Miss West out after curfew last night, my sincere apologies. To both of you." He bowed deeply. "I would like you to keep the breach to yourself, Tariq. My parents went through enough yesterday. They don't need to know I had one of the guests out of their rooms in violation of the rules."

"I understand." Tariq returned the bow. Then his laser-like gaze flicked over me. "About this guest. What is she going to say about being the only candidate from Settlement Four?"

"She will say nothing, as it's nothing to do with her." The prince stepped toward me protectively, and I caught a whiff of his scent again.

Tariq nodded, the picture of deference. "Of course, Your Highness. What about the other girl? What steps are being taken?"

The prince's shoulders sagged. "Eve has no family to notify. The poor girl's an orphan. Once she's feeling better, I'll explain that she's welcome to remain here with us for as long as she likes. The palace will be her home if she chooses to stay here."

I had a million questions about that, but I kept my mouth shut.

"Very well," Tariq said. "Should we bring in a backup candidate from Settlement Four to replace her?"

The prince scrubbed a hand across his face. "I was thinking about it. I don't want to bring attention to the fact that Eve isn't participating. We need to rethink the launch. The televised portion, at least. I want it to be seamless, without giving the audience any reason to panic." He shook his head. "I feel terrible about what happened to the girl. I wanted this contest to be a reason for the settlements to unite."

"We can still do that. I give you my word that we will." Tariq rubbed his hands together then started pacing. "What if we eliminate the first round of the competition and leave that portion un-televised? We could prepare a montage to briefly narrate the events—"

"What's the first portion of the competition?" I asked.

Tariq kept pacing. "The prince was supposed to meet with each of the girls individually, several times, and then make the first cut at the end of next week. Fifteen girls will be going home."

The prince crossed his arms. "So you're saying we do the cut immediately?"

Tariq's eyes glittered. "Yes. I can prepare footage that includes Eve's arrival yesterday so there will be proof she was here. She can be listed as one of the contestants who didn't advance to the second round."

"And the other girls?"

Tariq waved the question away. "I can easily eliminate fourteen of the other girls. I'll spread it out among the settlements. This will be good, actually. I think we'll increase excitement by narrowing the field right away. And I'll make sure all the girls who are going home have crystal-clear instructions about what they can and cannot say about the experience."

The prince nodded. "Very good."

Tariq pointed at me. "One more thing. I think we need to make sure that Miss West advances. The viewers from Settlement Four will be so enthralled to have one of their own continuing in the contest that they'll never question why the other girl got cut in the first round. Do you have any objection to that?"

The prince glanced at me. Did I imagine it, or did he look tense?

"*I* don't have a problem with that." I had a lot of other problems, but advancing in the competition after making so many blunders wasn't one of them. "Do you?" I asked the prince.

"Not at all." He smiled, forcing me to confront that dimple. "Just try not to pass out."

Blushing, I took the opportunity to smooth my immaculately ironed dress.

"I want to make sure she's featured heavily," Tariq said, "to throw them off the scent."

The prince turned to him. "Fine by me."

Tariq beamed at me, still rubbing his hands together. "Then, Miss West, congratulations. You've officially survived the first round."

As they discussed the details further, I pondered whether I should laugh or cry.

CHAPTER 10
ABOUT LAST NIGHT

THE PRINCE HELD OUT HIS ARM. "I'LL ESCORT YOU TO THE common room."

Tariq watched me from under his long eyelashes as I accepted the prince's offer. "I'll see you shortly, in our first class." He nodded, then sidled off.

I waited until his footsteps disappeared down the hall. "Thank you for saving me from him."

"Any time." The prince smiled. "The royal emissary's been with my family for a long time. He's been pushing for us to do something like this, and he's thrilled about the contest. He's particularly thrilled about *running* the contest. It's my responsibility to show him that I'm still the boss."

"I think you made that clear."

"I hope so. I have to keep him on a short leash, lest he scare you and the other girls off."

"He's just intense." I shrugged. "I'm not afraid of him."

The prince gave me a quick look. "I wasn't suggesting you should be. But watch your step, and don't underestimate him. He'll be paying close attention."

"Yes, Your Highness."

He frowned as he led me down the hall. "Would it be too bold of me to ask you to use my given name?"

The Dark Prince? "Do you mean Dallas?" It sounded funny on my lips.

"That's right."

"Are you named after the old American city?" That had been the topic of much speculation in the settlements, but none of us knew for sure.

"Yes. It was in one of the larger states."

I nodded. "Texas."

Dallas smiled at me. "That's right. My parents believe some of our ancestors came from there."

"Really?" I didn't know vampires had lived in the old America. But…had the Blacks *always* been vampires? Or did they have human ancestors?

How exactly did this whole vampire thing work?

I bit back the question. I had a million more, and none of them were particularly appropriate.

We continued down the hall, arms still linked, and I tried to ignore the feel of his muscled forearm. I could smell him again. *For the love of all things holy, do all vampires smell this good?*

My cheeks burned. *Get a grip, Gwyn.*

We reached the stairs, and Dallas paused. "I know you're curious about your friend, and I wanted to give you what information I can."

"Thank you, Your—Dallas. I mean, not *your* Dallas. Just Dallas." I bit my lip, willing myself to calm down so I stopped blathering. I needed to hear about Eve.

"I understand." He smiled kindly. "You've been through a lot in a short amount of time."

I sighed. "Thank you. But… How is she?"

He peered down the stairs, making sure no one was coming. "I have good news. Eve made it through the night.

Her fever's come down, and she's sleeping. It won't be long now."

My breath caught in my throat. "What won't be long?"

Keeping his voice low, he said, "She is turning from human to vampire. She won't exactly be different when the transformation is complete, but she won't be the same, either."

"How will she be different?"

The sun shone brightly through the windows, and I gasped. "Wait a minute. Should you be up right now?" The question sounded borderline hysterical, but I had my reasons.

He laughed. "You have nothing to fear from me, Gwyneth. I'm perfectly capable of moving about in the daytime, and I'm not going to bite. I promise."

"I'm sorry." Ashamed, I exhaled shakily. "Can all vampires withstand the sun?"

His smile vanished. "No, they cannot. And that's why we maintain certain rules here at the palace. But I'm sorry. We should keep this conversation focused on Eve."

"Of course." Still, I was pleased to have another piece of vampire intel to file away. "About Eve. What will she...eat?"

The prince watched me carefully. "Blood. And a fair amount of wine, I'm guessing. It's quite an adjustment."

My mind whirled. Eve *hated* vampires. And yet, when she awoke, that would be her new life. "Can you reverse the transformation?"

"No. The change is permanent."

We looked at each other for a moment.

"I know this isn't what she'd choose for herself," Dallas said. "But I promise you, I will take care of her. She won't be alone, and she won't suffer."

"Will you find food for her? Or will she have to hunt?" I refused to let a picture form in my mind.

"We have everything she'll need. And I promise it's all very sanitized and civilized. She won't be hurting anyone. All of our blood comes from donations."

"Oh. From the…staff?"

"And other sources. But I can assure you she'll have the best medical care and transformation guides. Everyone on the royal staff is well-equipped to deal with these sorts of situations. They're rare these days, but we're quite capable."

"You say it's rare—do you mean, for a vampire to bite a human?"

"Of course, it's rare." He tilted his chin and examined me. "Do you think I'm a savage?"

"No, but your mother could probably work on her table manners." I clapped a hand over my mouth as soon as the words tumbled out, cursing myself.

But Dallas threw his head back and laughed. "That's a good one, Gwyn."

I twisted my hands together, miserable. "I should never have said it."

His big shoulders stopped shaking as he calmed down. "Probably not. But I'm not used to people speaking freely in front of me."

Because it's likely a very, very bad idea. "It was rude of me. I'm so sorry."

"It's refreshing to be around someone with a different perspective, who isn't plotting and scheming and on their guard all the time." His expression sobered. "I wonder if the other contestants will be so forthcoming. I rather doubt it."

Crud. I *needed* to be plotting and scheming and on my guard all the time! This was a contest, and I was trying to win. So why did I keep saying the terribly inappropriate things that popped into my head? The other girls would probably dazzle him with calm demeanors, sentences that made sense, and pretending to be perfectly at home with a palace full of vampires.

I seriously suck at this.

Dallas leveled me with a look, as if he could read my thoughts. "It's okay if you don't want to be here. I understand."

"No, no. I *want* to be here." I swallowed hard, heart thudding. "I'm sorry for what I said. It's nothing personal. What happened last night frightened me."

"Of course, it did." He pursed his lips, his face stormy. If I hadn't upset him with the comment about his mother, I'd managed to do it just now. "I couldn't expect you to overlook something like that."

"Will Eve be able to stay out during the day, like you?" I asked, anxious to change the subject.

"I don't know yet," Dallas admitted. "Each transformation is different, and our kind evolves at an individual pace. Eve will be unique in many ways. We'll just have to wait and see what she's like in her new life."

"Will she have her same memories?"

"Many of them. Strong memories come through, but many of the details of everyday life become blurry."

"Like what?" In spite of myself, I was fascinated.

"My friend Lucas was turned. He always regretted that he couldn't remember what a cheeseburger tasted like, or why he'd enjoyed them so much."

"Is Lucas here?" I asked.

His eyes darkened further. "No, he's not. But enough of all this. We can't have you out past curfew *and* late for your first meal. Tariq will see me flailed." He held out his hand for mine. "Shall we?"

THE GUARDS STARED STRAIGHT AHEAD AS DALLAS SWEPT ME INTO the foyer and down the hall toward the common room. I could hear the other girls inside, eating their breakfast and talking amongst each other.

We paused outside the door, and I swallowed hard.

"What is it?" he asked.

"Nothing. I haven't really spoken with any of the other girls, is all." My nerves thrummed as I tried to gather my courage. Being thrust into a situation with a large group of strangers was *not* my thing.

"But you have friends back home?" Dallas asked.

I nodded. "Two." *Tavi, who's on her honeymoon with a husband she barely knows. Lyra, who's probably cursing me for coming here. As if I had a choice!*

"Two's something."

"And my family." I'd do well to remember them. I adjusted the collar of my dress as if I were adjusting armor.

His gaze flicked to my gown. "You have nothing to worry about. You look perfect. Stunning, actually."

My cheeks flamed again. "Thank you, Your—Dallas." I smiled at him, trying to make a joke, but his brow stayed furrowed in a deep V.

"And you have a sense of humor, albeit a mildly inappropriate one. You also just survived your first night in a den of vampires. You can probably survive a bunch of girls, don't you think?" He arched an eyebrow, all cool formality, where he'd been warm and protective earlier.

I'm royally screwing this up. Pun absolutely intended, ha ha.

He eyed me indifferently, and I tried to keep the disappointment from my face. "Of course."

But as he opened the door, I didn't feel certain about that or anything else.

CHAPTER 11
POP

ALL THE GIRLS STOPPED TALKING, STARING AT ME THEN AT DALLAS then back again.

Eve's words came back to me. *You have met other girls before, haven't you?*

"Well, good luck, then," Dallas said in a low voice.

He bowed and took his leave.

Coward. I was left standing solo, with forty-eight girls giving me disdainful side-eyes. I wanted to explain that I was no threat to them, but I didn't dare.

A kitchen maid rescued me, taking me to a seat in a far corner and pouring me tea. "Are you hungry, miss?"

"Not really." Still reeling from the missteps I'd just made with the prince, I was shaking.

She patted me kindly on the shoulder. "I'll get you some toast. You'll have your lessons all morning, so you need to eat."

I nodded, relieved that she was taking care of me when I didn't feel capable of it. I stirred some milk and honey into my tea then took a sip. *Mmm.* I couldn't remember the last time I'd had honey. The tea warmed me, giving me some strength back.

The kind maid brought my toast, and I slathered butter, another luxury, onto it.

I ate as delicately as I could manage, examining the other girls from the safety of my corner.

With the addition of the western settlers, the sheer volume of contestants seemed overwhelming. I barely recognized anyone from the day before. The girls were transformed by their beautiful dresses, elaborately arranged hair, and glistening jewels. They whispered to each other, intermittently looking in my direction, until one finally stood up and came over.

She was very tall, with blond braids wrapped around her head and a sour look on her face. In her ruby gown, she should've looked beautiful, but her disdainful expression marred her good looks.

I motioned to the chair across from me. "Would you like to sit?"

"I don't think so." She scowled down at me. "I'm just here to find out if you have news about the other girl from your settlement. Everyone wants to know."

"I don't know anything. Not yet."

She crossed her arms over her chest. "So what were you doing with the prince just now?"

"He showed me to the common room."

Her eyes flashed. "He didn't show *me* to the common room. Or any of the other girls."

"Oh."

Not getting any answers, she gave me one last nasty glare. With a flick of her braids, she turned on her heel and was gone.

"I'm Gwyneth, by the way. Settlement Four. Very nice to meet you," I mumbled to myself.

The maid brought me more toast and, no longer caring

what the other girls thought, I greedily stuffed it into my mouth.

I wanted to call the vinegary blonde back to my table and tell her, through a mouthful of toast, that the Dark Prince was all hers. He wasn't interested in me and my unruly mouth, and I wasn't interested in *him*, his fangs, his mood swings, or his godforsaken mother.

Talk about the mother-in-law from hell.

But of course, I said nothing. I couldn't be a coward, and I could no longer be honest. I'd made it through the first cut by sheer luck. It might've even been bad luck, I couldn't be sure.

Still, I had to collect myself and get back in the running for the prince's heart.

I need to win to save my family.

Even if winning meant lying to everyone and turning my back on what my father and brother had fought for. Even if it meant a death sentence instead of a new life for me.

So be it.

THE BREAKFAST DISHES WERE CLEARED BY THE TIME TARIQ AND HIS band of sentinels appeared. He smiled approvingly at us in our finery. "Ladies, please follow me to the salon. We'll begin our first lesson shortly."

To my dismay, he fell into step beside me as we proceeded down the hall. "Miss West," he said tightly, "is everything all right?"

"Everything's fine." I tried to keep my face a smooth mask, even as girls around us looked at me curiously. *Just great.* I didn't need any more attention. "Can I help you with something?"

He adjusted his tunic. "I just want to make sure that everything I said this morning was clear, and that you understand your position and your duty to the royal family."

A million questions dangled on the tip of my tongue, but I remembered what Dallas had said. *He'll be watching your every step.*

"Yes, my lord. I'm here to follow the contest rules to the letter. It's very important to me. I came here to represent my district well." His eyes briefly locked with mine, both of us thinking of Settlement Four's other candidate, whose story had gone decidedly off-script.

He nodded formally. "And I appreciate that, Miss West. See you in the salon."

He walked away, and the girl next to me eyed me worriedly. "Are you all right? Everyone seems to be fussing about."

"Yes. I'm fine."

She smiled kindly. "I'm so sorry about what happened to the other girl from your district."

My shoulders sagged. "Thank you. I'm sorry too."

The girl held out her hand and shook mine firmly. "I'm Shaye. I'm from Twenty-Four, on the western border."

"Wow, you traveled far."

She nodded as we filed into the salon. "We drove non-stop." She selected a small sofa toward the back and motioned for me to join her. I sank down, relieved that I had someone to sit with.

Shaye arranged her tangerine silk dress around her. She had thick, tawny ringlets that hung halfway down her back, enormous brown eyes, burnished-copper skin, and enviable curves. She was, as my mother would say, a showstopper.

"What did they use for transport?" I asked.

"A bus." She leaned forward conspiratorially. "They had backup fuel for it onboard, lots of it."

"Wow." None of the settlements had access to fuel or vehicles since the war. The Black Guard had taken all of it and made using public transportation mandatory. In our settlement, we walked everywhere. When I went to the market, I pulled a wagon to hold my wares. Traveling great distances was out of the question.

Shaye watched as Tariq stalked to the front of the room. "It's been an eye-opener, all right, even though I missed what happened last night. Everyone's talking about it, though. Did the girl...did she make it?" She shivered.

"I'm not sure." I didn't want to lie, but I didn't know what the truth was. *Would Eve still be Eve?*

Shaye's face pinched. "It's so sad. And I have to admit I was surprised. I didn't know about them. I mean, I didn't know for sure what they are."

I sighed. "None of us did. Like you said, this has all been an eye-opener."

"Some of the other girls said the royals were nocturnal. But the prince escorted you this morning. How does it all *work*?"

"He said only some of them can't come out during the day. He can."

"So strange..." She shook her head then obediently closed her mouth and focused on the royal emissary.

Relieved to be next to someone who followed the rules without making a fuss, I immediately felt guilty. *Eve didn't deserve what she got.*

"Ladies." Tariq paused his pacing long enough to address us. "As you know, there's been a situation. The royal family and I have discussed it at length, and we are going to be making some updates to the Pageant's process."

Everyone started talking at once until he frowned. Silence settled over the crowd. "We will be making the first round of cuts today, first thing this morning."

Again, the room erupted into worried whispers.

"I can assure you, this has been given very delicate thought. I appreciate your cooperation in this matter. Now, I have a list of names. If I call you, please take a seat at the conference table. I'll be with you shortly."

Tariq quickly announced fourteen girls' names. Each one rose, cheeks flushed, and took a seat at the large table.

Unfortunately, the tall girl with the braids wasn't among them.

I felt sorry for the girls, some of whom looked close to tears But they were *free*. Free from this place, free from the vampires, free from pretending to be happy to be here.

"It's a shame," Shaye said, breaking my reverie. "They're going home to nothing, with nothing to show for this, not even a fair chance. I'm sure they're all disappointed."

"Maybe they're relieved."

"Relieved to go back home and resume starving? I kind of doubt it." Shaye frowned as one of the girls started crying.

Tariq joined them at the table, speaking softly and offering tissues. Then he pulled out a dossier of documents, which he handed around.

"What do you think those are?" Shaye asked.

A redheaded girl who'd been sitting behind us suddenly leaned forward, putting her face between ours, and making me jump. "Probably some sort of non-disclosure agreement so they don't rat out the royal family."

"Huh." Shaye shrugged. "You'd think the royals would do something nice for them. It's not as if they don't have enough to go around." Her gaze traveled from the gold enamel on the couch's intricately carved arm to the luxurious Oriental rug and the heavy, elegant drapes that adorned the floor-to-ceiling windows.

"It'll be nice if they don't snack on them before they leave," muttered the redhead.

Shaye and I looked at each other. "Don't talk to us," we said in unison.

The girl scowled but moved back into her own seat.

"I don't know about you," Shaye said, "but I think we're already in enough trouble without that sort of talk."

"I'm in complete agreement." Relieved that I'd found someone with a similar disposition, I said, "They should do something nice for these girls, I agree. I don't know if anyone but the winner gets a prize, but it would be lovely if they were given something that could help their families."

"It would soften the blow." Shaye shrugged. "Unfortunately, we aren't in charge."

A woman in her mid-forties sailed through the door, ending our discussion. She was short and plump but so poised that she seemed six feet tall. She stopped at the front of the room and cleared her throat.

"Girls, I'm Ms. Blakely, and I'm here for your instruction." She nodded at us over her half-moon spectacles, prim and proper in her nubby off-white skirt suit. "This morning, we are going through sensitivity training. There will be a test afterward, so pay attention."

The redhead groaned, but Shaye and I didn't say a word. We just listened.

Ms. Blakely began the lesson, outlining the proper steps when meeting someone for the first time.

"It's imperative to ask them their name and try to get the pronunciation right, even if it's difficult. Do you have difficulty pronouncing certain types of names? Well then, try saying them more often! You'd be amazed what you can accomplish when you make other people's well-being a priority."

Mrs. Blakely clasped her hands together. "Another thing you might want to consider is making eye contact. If the person you're speaking with seems open to it, you can shake their hand or reach out and touch them gently. Read the signals they give you."

She took a step toward us. "We may look different on the outside. We may indeed be from different places, eat different things, and believe in different gods. We might not speak the same or dress the same. But I can assure you, on the inside, we are all more alike than we are different."

The redhead snorted, but I ignored her. Instead, I listened raptly to the information about how to get along with vampires.

It was a subject I couldn't afford to fail.

WE WERE GIVEN A MIDMORNING BREAK AND ALLOWED TO TAKE A brief walk on the eastern grounds. I left the salon with Shaye and ran into my guard, whom I hadn't seen in what felt like days.

He nodded at me. Remembering his admonition not to speak to him, I only nodded in return.

"Your guards will escort you around the grounds," Tariq announced. "And maids are waiting at the entrance with wraps to wear. Please dress accordingly."

Shaye's guard came and stood at attention. We collected our cloaks and went outside, our sentinels following close behind.

Even in the early winter, the eastern garden was astounding. No flowers bloomed, but the meticulously kept grounds were stunning in and of themselves. The green grasses were still lush, and the bushes artfully trimmed. Large, square reflecting pools ran the length of the gardens, reflecting the sky.

"This is gorgeous." Shaye stopped, breathing in deeply and closed her eyes for a moment. "And it feels so good to be outside. That bus ride lasted forever."

"What is Settlement Twenty-Four like?" I asked. "Besides far away?"

"It's lush, like this. We have lots of trees, and it rains often. I live outside the city, and where we are—well, let's just say it's pretty rustic." She laughed. "We don't have indoor plumbing kind of rustic. The palace is quite a change."

"Do you live with your family?"

Shaye's eyes darkened. "My mother and my sisters. My father and brothers enlisted…"

I nodded. "Mine too." I reached out and squeezed her hand. "We don't need to talk about it here."

With a grateful nod, she turned, and we continued down the path. "I was surprised to see how many humans work here." Shaye kept her voice neutral.

"As was I. I had no idea."

We reached the edge of the final pool and looped around, heading back toward the palace. From this vantage, the building was even more impressive. Massive, curved windows looked out on the garden, the windows reflecting the beauty and light of the park.

She stopped. "I can't believe I'm actually here. It's like I'm dreaming."

"I know. Can you imagine living like this?" I gestured toward the palace.

Shaye smiled. "Whoever wins will live here. And although a lot of this isn't ideal, it *is* the opportunity of a lifetime."

CHAPTER 12
THE FLASH

THE DOORS TO THE PALACE OPENED, AND A ROW OF GUARDS marched out, lining up on either side of the path. The prince strode out next, nodding as they saluted.

Shaye and I watched as he made a beeline for Tariq. The two men spoke for a minute, and I increased my pace. I wanted to see if I could catch Dallas's eye, to speak with him about the contestants who'd been cut.

We got closer, and I noticed the other girls nearby, all watching the prince carefully. There seemed to be a sudden increase in giggling and hair tossing, which made me want to vomit.

Dallas glanced my way, then excused himself from Tariq. "Miss West, why are you frowning again?"

I composed my features even as Shaye's jaw dropped at his easy familiarity. "I'm not." I forced myself to smile at him. "May we speak with you for a moment?"

His gaze flicked to Shaye, and he bowed deeply. "You must be Miss Iman. It's a pleasure make your acquaintance."

"Your Highness." Shaye curtsied flawlessly, and I tried not be jealous of her lithe grace.

"What can I do for you?" Dallas seemed back in good humor. He smiled at us winningly, every inch the perfect prize.

"Miss Iman and I were wondering—will the girls who've been cut be given anything? Any sort of…separation package?"

He cocked his head. "I don't know what you mean."

I clasped my hands together. "It's just that they've come here from nothing, with only high hopes. And now they're going home without anything to show for it—not even a full week of meals. It would be nice if they received some sort of compensation. A goodwill gesture from the royal family, if you will."

He nodded, his brow furrowed in thought. "That's an excellent idea."

"It was Miss Iman's, actually."

Shaye blushed noticeably as Dallas smiled at her. "Thank you, miss. My family and I are working on our outreach and support of the settlements. Insight like this is extremely helpful."

"Their families will appreciate any help you can give them. The rations aren't enough for most." I nodded. "It would go a long way, I imagine."

Dallas looked surprised. "Do their families suffer?"

I raised my chin. "A good many of them."

He cursed under his breath then turned on his heel. "I'll speak with you two later." He stormed off, Tariq nipping at his heels like a well-kept and demanding chihuahua.

"What was that all about?" Shaye asked. "Have you spoken with His Highness often? He seemed quite familiar with you."

"We've talked before." I didn't say more.

"So? Doesn't he know the conditions of his own kingdom?" She frowned. "He seems a bit clueless."

"That was interesting, wasn't it? He seemed genuinely surprised. I don't know *what* he knows." As I watched his broad back retreat, I wondered if certain realities were being kept from the Dark Prince.

❧

After we finished Mrs. Blakely's test, we took a break for lunch. I was thrilled to have a friend in Shaye. We ate together and sat next to each other throughout the afternoon's lectures. It was a relief to have an ally, particularly a kind, smart one.

The girls who'd been cut weren't present during the afternoon class. I wondered if they'd already been sent home.

We were directed to our rooms before dinner. I gladly collapsed onto my bed, enjoying the peace after a long day. The fire crackled, and I sank back against my pillows, my eyelids drooping.

There was a knock at the door. "Miss?" Evangeline's perky voice chimed. "May we come in?"

"Of course." I tried to keep the resentment out of my voice. My maids were the best. Plus, *maids*.

Evangeline, Bria, and Bettina filed in. Bettina made a beeline for me, clucking as she fluffed my hair, smoothed my dress, and pinched my cheeks.

"Ow!"

She grinned at me. "The prince is coming. Stand up, miss! And please don't say blasphemous things this time. Or faint." She winked as I rolled my eyes.

"What does he want?" I huffed, but another knock on the door silenced me.

"Yes, Your Highness?" asked Evangeline.

"May I come in?"

"Of course, Your Highness."

Dallas came through the door, tall and almost painfully handsome in his steel-gray tunic. Still, he had a dark, brooding look, as if he'd been mulling over what Shaye and I had told him all afternoon.

Oh boy. Here we go.

"Evangeline. Bria. Bettina." He nodded to them, and they curtsied, facing flushing at his use of their names.

His dark eyes flashed to me. "Miss West."

I crossed my arms over my chest. "I thought we were on a first name basis at least in private, *Dallas*."

Evangeline looked at me, shocked, then quickly composed her features.

He raked a hand through his hair, making it stand up in spiky waves. "I spoke with my advisors about the young women who were cut. We've decided to offer each of their families a generous stipend for letting their daughters participate in the contest. Each remaining girl will also be awarded a similar stipend when it's their time to return home."

When he told me the amount of money involved, I put a hand over my heart. "That's very kind."

He smiled a bit sheepishly. "Is that an acceptable amount for a family? I'm afraid I don't really have much to compare it to. The Northern monetary system was quite different, and my staff has been assuring me for years that the rations we administered to the settlements were more than generous."

"They aren't." For once, I wasn't ashamed to speak my mind. He needed to know the truth.

Dallas cursed under his breath.

"But what you're doing will make an *enormous* difference in most of our lives. Even those of us who had wealth before the war are running out. Honestly, I can't thank you enough. I don't know what to say." I exhaled shakily, imagining the look on my mother's face when she learned of the money coming our way.

"Please don't pass out," Dallas said cautiously.

"I won't, I promise. I was just imagining how thrilled my mother will be."

His face relaxed into a smile, and it was like the sun coming out. "That's at least one upside of all this."

"What do you mean?"

The glower returned. "I'm not pleased with my staff's misrepresentations. I'm replacing several of my advisors. Heads will roll for this."

I swallowed hard.

Dallas's shoulders sagged. "Not literal heads, Gwyn."

"Of course not," I fake-scoffed.

He rose to go. "You still think I'm a savage."

"A generous one." I smiled. "Thank you for what you've done."

He bowed deeply. "I look forward to seeing you tomorrow."

"As do I."

As I watched him go, I wondered if I'd just broken one of my rules again—and told the truth.

CHAPTER 13
A GLIMMER IN THE DARK

WE HAD LESSONS DAY IN AND DAY OUT. FOR SOME UNGODLY reason, we were doing academic classes—geography, spelling, handwriting, and arithmetic. Later in the week, we'd be learning posture exercises. Tariq kept pestering us to stand up straight. He'd threatened us with six-inch spiked high heels and an obstacle course if we didn't shape up.

Next week, we'd begin spending more time with the prince, and the Pageant would begin in earnest. For now, it was lessons all day, every day. Tariq said he wanted us in top form for the first televised round of the competition.

I refused to think about the impending cameras. I would probably trip, pass out, and blurt out inappropriate insults on live television.

So excited. No, really.

I'd only seen Dallas in passing. Each time, he'd given me a deep bow and a distracted smile. I hadn't heard another word from him about Eve, and I hadn't caught a glimpse of her.

At the end of another long day, replete with back-to-back classes and no news, I trudged to my room. No matter what, I was grateful to have a warm fire and a full belly, two things I'd been sorely lacking at home.

I shivered, thinking of my family. I hadn't gotten a letter from them yet, and I vowed to write them the next day. So much had happened in my short time at the palace. Perhaps it was for the best that my letter would be censored—what on Earth would I tell them?

Dear Mom,
Having a great time at the palace with the royal family. By the way, they're all vampires! They can drink our blood and change us into their kind! The queen ended my friend's human life the very first day!
Still hoping I win?
All My Best,
Gwyn

I would probably just stick to details about how pretty the palace was and about the meals. Definitely.

I changed into my nightgown and gratefully crept into bed. I fell instantly into a heavy sleep.

I dreamt of the queen. She and the king had been absent from our daily schedules, and I'd wondered if they'd keep it that way. I certainly hoped so. But she was in my dream. I couldn't escape her inside my own head.

The queen's long, white-blonde hair flowed behind her as she sailed down the grand staircase. Her dress was the same as that first night—sky blue, with a blood stain at the hip.

She reached the bottom of the stairs and came toward me, arms outstretched. As she drew closer, I could see blood trickling from her mouth. There were footsteps on the stairs, and then my father and brother appeared, staggering down after her. They were both pale, deathly pale, with fang marks in their necks. They reached out for me—

"NO!" I sat up straight, sweat coating me, breathing hard.

I clutched the blankets to my chest. *Just a dream, Gwyn. A nightmare.*

I had a sip of water, then got up and stoked the fire. My hands were still shaking, but I willed myself to calm down.

They aren't dead. You don't know for sure.

But my heart ached. I didn't know if I'd ever see them again, outside of my dreams.

I went to the window and stared outside, watching the stars as they winked against the blackness. When I thought of Father and Balkyn, my heart felt like one of those stars—hopeful in the dark, a spark against all the odds.

Out of the corner of my eye, I caught a flash of movement. I looked toward the grounds, and I saw it again—a glimmer of white.

"What in the bloody hell is *that*?"

A figure appeared, walking alone on the manicured lawn in the darkness. Her long white shift trailed out behind her. Her alabaster skin reflected the moonlight. She stopped and looked up at me, aqua eyes burning fiercely bright in the darkness.

Eve.

Our gazes locked. Someone shouted something from down below. She took off running but was intercepted by a large, dark figure.

Whoever he was, he led her back toward the castle. She struggled against him.

Was she okay? Was that a friend or foe leading her back here?

I paced back and forth, wondering if I dared risk leaving my room after curfew again. *If Tariq finds out...* But alone in the dark, I couldn't lie to myself. I needed to know if my friend was okay.

I grabbed my robe and tied it tightly. Taking a deep breath, I stole from my chambers.

The lights flickered dimly in the hall. I crept toward the stairs, listening for any noise, any sign that I was about to be caught.

But there was nothing, only an eerie silence, punctuated by the thudding of my heart.

At the top of the stairs, I stopped to listen again. Nothing. I'd made it halfway down when voices drifted up from the foyer.

"You shouldn't try to do too much. Your body's still dealing with a lot." *Dallas.*

"I…I saw her." A voice, gravelly but familiar. *Eve.*

"She's asleep. But if I can arrange it, I'll bring her to you soon."

"I want… I want…" Eve started crying.

At that, I tore down the stairs.

"Gwyneth!" Dallas yelled. "Stop right there." Even in the darkness, I could see the strain on his face.

I obeyed, staying on where I was, as Eve whirled toward me.

She was different. Her skin glowed in the dim light of the candles, pale, luminescent alabaster. Her aqua eyes glowed as if lit from within. She took a step toward me, reaching out with one hand.

Come to me. I heard her voice in my head.

I took a step closer.

Dallas moved protectively toward me, inserting himself between us. "Gwyneth. *Please.*"

Eve peered around him, aqua eyes beseeching me. *I miss you…help me! There's so much pain. I'm in so much pain!*

My heart fisted. "Oh, Eve. I'm so sorry."

Eve tried to get past Dallas, but he wrapped his arms around her. She fought him, but he didn't budge. "Guards!"

Five sentinels appeared immediately. "Escort Miss West to her room *now.* Lock her door, and guard her room tonight. Make sure she's safe or your heads will roll. Go!"

Eve still reached for me. I reached back as the guards hustled me up the stairs.

I heard her sobbing as they dragged me away.

CHAPTER 14
PERSUASION

"What's wrong?" Shaye asked me the next morning at breakfast.

"Nothing," I mumbled.

Her brow furrowed in worry. "Your eyes look puffy. You can tell me, you know. But you don't have to talk if you don't want to."

I grabbed a blueberry muffin and inspected it. "I had a nightmare. I woke up crying." It was at least part of the truth.

"I get them too," she said. "Ever since my family went off to war."

I buttered the muffin and ate it. No matter what horrors befell me at the castle, ever since I'd tasted that first splendid toast, I refused to skip a meal.

"How many siblings do you have?" I asked.

"Four. Two brothers who left for the war with my father, and my younger sisters at home. You?"

"Three. Balkyn, my older brother, went to fight with my father. Then I have Winnie and Remy. They're little. They're still home with my mom."

Shaye nodded. "It's been hard not knowing if they're

coming home, but we've managed. I never thought I'd learn how to skin an animal, but I can do it fast now. Especially squirrels." She shivered. "Even though it's totally gross."

"You're braver than me. All I did at home was barter our china away for firewood."

She shrugged. "At least you had china to barter. We were poor to begin with, so…"

Tariq came in then, looking polished and formal in a deep purple tunic, his hair gelled into a reflective helmet. "Ladies. We will begin our morning lesson shortly, but I have news. Today begins the first meetings with the prince."

The room erupted, the girls chattering excitedly.

"I will notify you when it's your turn. He will take each girl for a stroll on the grounds or for tea. When your time alone is finished, he will escort you back to your lesson." He nodded curtly. "As you were."

Shaye sighed. "Well, it will be good to get this out of the way."

"What do you mean?"

"They'll make more cuts after this. I bet a lot of us will be going home after he meets with us one-on-one."

I frowned. "Based on one turn around the park?"

"You can tell like *that*"—Shaye snapped her fingers —"whether you have chemistry with somebody. Either His Highness is going to feel it, or he isn't, and that will be the end of that."

"I don't think he's basing his choices on attraction only."

"Of course not." Shaye took another muffin and slathered butter on it. Like me, she didn't pass up any opportunity to enjoy the palace's scrumptious food. She waited until she'd swallowed before she continued. "But this will be the easy part for him. Cut first on attraction, and then things get a bit more convoluted."

"What do you mean?" I grabbed another muffin too.

Shaye looked thoughtful. "The prince will have to figure out who's the most appropriate match. Who can help him politically, who can get along with his family, who can help him unite the settlements behind the throne. It will be more difficult than figuring out who he wouldn't mind kissing."

For some reason, my cheeks heated. "Do you think he'll be…kissing the girls? To figure out if he likes them that way?"

"Who knows? He's the prince. He can do whatever he wants." She tossed some more muffin into her mouth and shrugged. "But we should probably go brush our teeth after this just in case."

I swallowed over a sudden lump in my throat.

"Don't look so grim." Shaye swatted my hand. "He might be a lot of things, but ugly isn't one of them. You'll live."

As I followed her out of the room, I sorely hoped she was right.

I BRUSHED MY TEETH THREE TIMES IN A ROW. THEN I PINCHED MY own cheeks before I went back downstairs, inwardly cursing myself. *Stupid, stupid, stupid.*

But at least worrying about my breath kept my thoughts from my haunting encounter with Eve.

I spread out my violet frock as I sat down next to Shaye, smoothing it. She winked at me as the lesson began.

I frowned then listened as Mrs. Blakely talked to us about proper table manners.

Tariq came in a moment later. He tapped one of the other girls on the shoulder, and she jumped up, following him in an excited flourish.

I tried not to pay attention to Tariq's periodic entries into the salon, just like I tried to keep from examining each girl when they came back. One appeared flushed and happy, and another very pretty girl with straight black hair was positively beaming when she returned.

The rude blonde with the braids looked sour as ever when she came back. I wondered if her meeting with the prince hadn't gone well, or if her face had permanently frozen in a look of disapproval.

We had lunch—a fabulous turkey and avocado salad, followed by fresh brownies—then returned to our lesson, but not before Shaye and I raced off to brush our teeth again. At least I wasn't alone in my ridiculousness.

Back in lessons, during which we were kept busy counting fork tines, Tariq came for two more girls.

Finally, when my eyes were crossed from glaring at silverware, he approached me. "Miss West."

Shaye winked at me, and I stuck my tongue out at her behind the royal emissary's back.

I'd rarely been so happy to see Tariq. I followed him dutifully out to the hall where Dallas stood, waiting.

We bowed to each other. As soon as Tariq stopped watching us, the prince took my arm and led me outside.

His jaw was taut. Once we were alone, he spoke, his voice tense. "I'm *very* upset with you—"

"You shouldn't be! She saw me from the grounds! She *looked* at me, Dallas! It was like she was calling to me—"

"Probably because she wanted to drain you dry." He tucked my arm closer against him, and I inhaled his heady scent. It made me dizzy on top of being defensive.

Dallas shook his head, leading me down the path by the pools. "She's not safe to be around yet. Don't you think I would've let you see her?"

"I don't know. I don't know what princely things you do all day, or if you'd forgotten all about me."

He stopped walking. "I assure you that I haven't forgotten you. You've insulted me more in a short period of time than anyone else I've ever known. You're not likely to slip my mind any time soon."

I bristled with guilt. "Sorry about that."

"Mm-hmm." Not sounding at all convinced, he pulled me down the path bordering the reflective pools. "Eve got out last night without my permission. She tricked the guards who were watching her and snuck outside. She's not ready to be on her own, and she's *not* ready to have unsupervised human company."

"Why not?"

He looked at me as if I'd sprouted three additional heads. "She's *hungry*. Starving, actually."

"Aren't you feeding her?"

Dallas blew out a deep breath. "I'm trying to. But she's rejecting the donated blood. This happens sometimes with the newly turned. They want to…hunt."

I shuddered, my hand crawling up toward my neck. "Did she want to hunt *me*?"

He winced. "It's instinct, Gwyn. You know she would never hurt you if she had any idea what she was doing. Her body's been through an enormous change. She's not in control of herself at all. She doesn't even know herself yet."

"Is that normal?"

He nodded. "It is. All transformations have an element of catastrophe to them."

"Did that happen to you?" I asked.

"I wasn't turned. I was born this way."

My jaw dropped. "Your parents…" My brow furrowed as I

attempted to stammer out a coherent question. "They had you after they'd..."

Dallas stopped in his tracks and took my hands. "Vampires, at least Northern ones, can have biological children, the way humans can. We can also create others of our kind the way Eve was created, by transformation."

"Wait—there are *other* vampires? Besides the northerners?"

His dark eyes flashed. "There are all sorts of creatures in the world, Gwyn."

I shivered. *Raised in a bubble, indeed.* Except my mother had no idea she'd been living in one too.

Unable to grasp the full impact of his words, I brought the subject back to Eve. "What will happen if she refuses to eat?"

"She'll give in eventually. The hunger will get the better of her."

"I know you said I shouldn't be around her, but can I see her?" I looked at him hopefully. "With you?"

"It's not safe—"

"Please, your—Dallas." I reached for his hands. "You will protect me. I just want her to know that I'm here and that I still care about her."

He took a step back and eyed me, from the bottom of my dress to the top of my head. "You're not an easy person to say no to. I'm not sure if that's a blessing or a curse."

"Thank you, your Dallas." I teased.

He grunted, but I caught a flash of his dimple. For some reason, pleasing him made my heart rate kick up.

As he escorted me back to my lesson, I wondered if *that* was a blessing or a curse.

CHAPTER 15
VISITING HOURS

DALLAS ARRANGED FOR ME TO MISS THE LAST SESSION OF THE DAY. The lecture was about distinguishing between different varieties of tea, and I wasn't sorry to miss it.

I *was* sorry I had to lie to Shaye—but the prince insisted. I told her my maids were fitting me for some new, television-worthy dresses and that I'd see her at dinner.

Dallas waited in the foyer. The late-afternoon sun shone through the grand windows, its glimmering rays layering the prince in hues of gold. I sucked in a breath when I saw him, praying he didn't notice the effect on me.

I wanted to advance in the contest, but I didn't want to be a besotted, doe-eyed *fool*. I had to keep my wits, as well as my spastic hormones, about me.

But the prince raked a hand through his hair and grinned as I came closer, inspecting my flushed cheeks. He missed nothing.

Dallas held out his arm for me. "Gwyneth."

I nodded curtly. "Dallas."

He pulled me against him, and I had to force myself not to react visibly. I could smell him, and I could feel his large, muscular frame next to me. Everything in my body went all quaky and haywire. *Why is that?* I'd dated loyal-to-a-fault Drew Baylor for almost a year, and I'd never once quivered in his presence. In fact, I'd found him quite dull.

Maybe the effect Dallas had on me was a vampire thing? Or a tall, dark, and royal thing?

"What are you thinking?" he asked, his brow furrowed. "You have a funny look on your face."

"Eve." I coughed. "I'm nervous."

He nodded. "It will be okay. I told her you were coming, but that I had to keep you separated."

"Okay." I vowed to keep my mind on my friend and her suffering, not my rioting hormones.

We were headed toward the medical ward, but Dallas suddenly turned the corner.

"You moved her?"

He nodded. "We thought she'd be more comfortable in private chambers. But she still has a full medical staff attending her."

He took me to a door guarded by two clearly vampiric sentinels. They bowed, and I curtsied in return. Typically, the vampire guards only worked at night, but perhaps it was safer for Eve to have her own kind protecting her.

Dallas opened the door. I tried to sniff one of the guards as we passed, but I couldn't tell whether he smelled as good as the prince.

The guard looked at me funny. I pretended not to notice.

Eve's chamber was stunning, with an enormous crystal chandelier and a white marble fireplace. Velvet tapestries of rich blue framed the floor-to-ceiling windows, and her four-poster bed was made from an elegant, intricately carved dark wood.

I walked in, looking around, but Dallas raised his hand to stop me. "Wait. Let me talk to her first. Eve?"

"What do you want?" Her sullen and scratchy voice came from…*inside the wardrobe?*

"Are you hiding again?" Dallas asked.

"It's not hiding. I'm taking a sabbatical from the freak show," Eve snapped.

"Gwyneth's here. I brought her to see you."

"Liar."

He chuckled. "I told you before that I won't ever lie to you."

"Liar," Eve said again. But the door creaked open.

I caught a flash of strawberry-blond curls, then her alabaster face peeked out.

Again, her eyes almost undid me. It was like they were battery-operated. Eve's aqua eyes glowed as they greedily raked over me. I forced myself not to flee the room.

She stepped out of the wardrobe, and I was surprised by her outfit, a dark tunic and pants, as if she were about to go riding or swing a sword around.

"Why is she dressed like that?" I asked Dallas.

"I can hear you, you know. I'm right here." Eve stalked closer, and Dallas put his body protectively in front of me.

"I know. I just didn't know if—"

"What?" Eve asked, peeking around Dallas. "If I still understood English?"

My shoulders sagged. "I thought I should ask the prince. I don't want to upset you."

"Are you worried I might bite?" Eve arched an eyebrow. *Or mess with your mind?*

"Hey! Whoa, whoa. How did you do that?" I put my fingers to my temples.

She grinned. "Just girl talk. One old friend to another."

"What did you do?" Dallas asked.

Eve stepped back and shrugged, some of her former jaunty swagger shining through. "Nothing, Your High-and-Mightiness."

Dallas turned back to me, eyes burning. "Tell me now, Gwyn."

Eve waggled her eyebrows. "It's Gwyn now, is it? I see you two have gotten quite cozy."

Dallas bit back a curse, keeping his eyes on me. "Tell me what she did, and tell me now."

"She spoke inside my head."

Eve crossed her arms over her chest. "Once a bootlicking Upper East Ender, always a bootlicking Upper East Ender."

"Bootlicking?" Dallas looked confused.

"I'm trying to help you," I said through clenched teeth.

"Help me? Help *me*?" Eve laughed, but it was a bleak sound, barren of joy.

I took a step forward, ignoring Dallas's warning look. "I'm still your friend. If you'll have a filthy bootlicking Upper East Ender as a friend, that is."

"I don't think I can have friends anymore. Can I, Dallas?"

"Of course, you can."

"Do *you* have any friends?" she asked him pointedly.

"Not here," he admitted. "But maybe that can change."

"Good luck." Eve rolled her eyes.

"How did you talk inside my head?" I asked.

"I don't know. You're the first one it's worked with." Eve frowned. "I can only talk in *your* head. I tried it with the guards, I tried it with Dallas, I tried it with the queen —nothing."

Dallas turned to her sharply. "Gwyneth can hear you because she's human. It's one of our kind's tricks. We can use it to hypnotize our…prey."

Eve looked thoughtful while I moaned.

Dallas stepped toward her. "But what did you mean about the queen? You've seen her?"

Eve's aqua eyes flashed. "I tried to mind-speak with her, but she didn't hear me."

"When?" Dallas's whole body went tense.

"Every night," Eve said. "She comes in when she thinks I'm asleep and plays with my hair. She coos and fusses over me like I'm a baby. It's *weird*."

Dallas's shoulders sagged. "It's because of my sister."

"You have a sister?" I asked.

His gaze met mine. "She died years ago. My mother's never gotten over it. She might be having…maternal instincts for Eve."

"Just what I freaking need! Your mother has some serious issues." Eve rubbed her neck. "*And* a wicked grip."

I laughed. "Dallas was right. You're not the same, but you're not completely different."

"It's not funny, Gwyn." Eve shook her head. "I'll never go home again. I can't."

The laughter died on my lips. "I know. I'm so sorry."

Her blazing eyes rose to meet mine. "You warned me to stop, to keep my mouth shut. But I didn't listen because I never do."

The three of us looked at each other, an awkward silence settling over us.

"What happens next?" I asked.

Dallas paced near the fire. "Eve will learn to drink donated blood so she gets her strength up. This will also prevent her from luring her friends closer so she can drain them dry." He looked at her pointedly.

Eve rolled her eyes. "I wasn't actually going to *bite* Gwyn."

Dallas jerked his thumb at me. "You smell her, right?"

"I'm sorry?" I asked, taken aback.

"Yes," Eve said dejectedly.

"She's mouthwatering. Of course, you would have bitten her."

I stamped my foot. "I *beg* your pardon!"

Dallas turned to me, amused. "It was a compliment. You smell fantastic. I usually have to guzzle a quart of blood before I come to see you just so I don't get too excited."

I looked at him, incredulous. "The way my blood smells gets you excited? Like you would be excited to have a roast for dinner?"

Dallas looked thoughtful. "I don't know about that. I've never had a roast."

Eve shook with silent laughter. I vowed to yell at her next.

I focused on the prince. "Oh, you're unbelievable. My point is, *that's* all you care about? My smell? I could be wearing a burlap sack instead of this dress, then!" I spluttered.

"I'm actually fond of the dress." He eyed me, his gaze traveling over me appreciatively.

"Oh *stop*." My cheeks heated, and I clenched my hands into fists. "This is ridiculous. Tariq keeps threatening me with high heels! He shouldn't bother. He should just be stuffing me with food so I'll be plump. A goose ready for your dinner!"

Dallas tilted his chin as he inspected me. "I've never had goose, either. But when you put it like that, it somehow seems appealing."

"You're unbelievable."

"And *you* are adorable when you're mad."

"I'm. Not. Mad."

Dallas winked at Eve. "Does she seem mad to you?"

Eve stopped laughing and nodded. "I agree. She's cute like this. You two are funny together."

Disgusted with both of them, I turned on my heel to leave.

I stopped when I reached the door. "Eve, it was good to see you. I'll come as often as the prince allows."

"Thank you." Her voice was soft, and I could tell she meant it. She wasn't laughing anymore.

"Gwyneth—" the prince started.

I just held up a finger, and then I shook it back and forth, the universal sign for no.

"The goose will see you later." I stomped from the room.

"I'm looking forward to it."

Dallas's laughter trailed out behind me, and I cursed him the whole way back to my room.

CHAPTER 16
THE PERFECT DRESS

I FRETTED ABOUT WHAT DALLAS HAD SAID FOR THE REST OF THE afternoon.

Did he mean it literally, that I was *mouthwatering*? What on Earth did that indicate, besides the obvious?

Did he want anything from me other than to drink my blood?

I had a serious physical reaction to Dallas's scent. But I didn't want to drink his blood. I wanted…well, I had no idea what I wanted.

Did Dallas intend to marry the winner of the Pageant? Or did he just want to have her for supper?

The answer would gauge how I was doing so far, compared to the rest of the contestants. But of course, I didn't know the answer.

My thoughts swirled as I ate dinner with Shaye. Refusing to linger on the subject, I tried to focus on our conversation.

"How was the tea tasting?"

She crinkled her nose. "Bloody boring. How was the fitting?"

"Fine." I stuffed another piece of popover into my mouth so I didn't have to lie more.

"I had my walk with the prince during the last ten minutes of the lecture." Shaye played with her curls absently, looking dreamy.

I nearly choked. "How did it go?"

She grinned. "Great! He's really very nice, don't you think?"

I swallowed hard. "He's something, all right."

My friend's brown eyes focused on me. "Do you like him or not?"

I sighed. "I don't know. Sometimes yes, sometimes no." *That* was the truth. "What about you?"

"I like him," she said without reserve.

For some reason, my heart lurched at her words.

Shaye shrugged. "I had my doubts about the competition, but I think the prince is a good catch. Not just because he's wealthy and powerful, but because he's interesting and kind. And let's face it—he's hot."

I put down my popover, feeling a bit sick. "He's handsome. Even I'll give him that."

"It's okay if you like him too," she said. "One of us might have to marry him. We should both be so lucky to like him."

I started tearing my napkin to shreds.

"Gwyn, what's wrong?"

"It's just that I don't want to like him." I lowered my voice. "I feel guilty because of my family. I feel like a traitor."

Shaye leaned forward. "We all feel like that just by being here. And we all knew it coming to the palace."

I nodded.

"The thing is," she continued, "we all came anyway because we didn't have a choice. And one of us must marry the prince no matter what. It's better to like him, don't you think?"

"Yes." I agreed with everything she said.

"Then why do you still look so miserable?"

Because you said you liked him.

"I'm just confused, I guess."

Shaye smiled at me. "That's good. That's how you know you're still human."

❧

I MULLED ABOUT MY ROOM AFTER DINNER. SEVERAL TIMES, I picked up the book I'd been trying to read then put it down. I paced in front of the fire. I had a sip of water.

I got back to pacing.

Shaye was my friend. So why was it that, when she said she liked the prince, I wanted to throw myself across the dinner table and scratch her eyes out?

I was just as bad as the vampires I pretended to loathe. I was an animal too, a beast.

A confused beast.

There was a knock at the door, and Evangeline stuck her pretty face into the room. "May I come in, miss? I have something for you."

"Of course."

She brought in a garment bag and hung it in the wardrobe. She unzipped it as she spoke. "The twins and I wanted you to have a special dress to wear for the first day of the televised program. We had the seamstresses whip up a little something."

She pulled it out, and I put a hand over my heart. "Oh, Evangeline. It's gorgeous!"

The gown was red satin. It glimmered with intricate beadwork sewn all over the bodice, which glittered in the firelight.

"Do you really like it?" Evangeline asked hopefully.

"I love it. It's stunning."

She beamed. "I think the prince will approve."

"I hope so." The words were out of my mouth before I could take them back.

Evangeline grinned. "He will. I'm happy to hear that you care what he thinks. Are you warming up to him a bit?"

I bit my lip. "I don't know. Maybe? He's trying to help my friend, Eve. I guess I saw another side of him."

"He really is a kind young man," she said. "I've never seen him be anything but fair with the staff."

"That's good to know." I nodded, refusing to feel guilty. Shaye was right, if I *had* to be here, it was better to approve of the prince.

"Now, let's try this on." Evangeline's eyes sparkled. "I want everything to be perfect for you."

I WOKE UP THE NEXT MORNING FEELING REFRESHED UNTIL I remembered Mira Kinney was coming today.

The cameras were coming today.

I cursed and pulled the blankets up over my head.

There was a knock at my door. "Miss," Bettina called, "I have your tea. And two letters."

I sat up immediately. "Come in."

She placed a tray on the table near the fire and smiled at me kindly. "One letter's from your family, and one's from the prince. Take your time waking up. It's still early. We'll be back in a little while to get you ready for your day."

"Thank you, Bettina." I caught a flash of her pink bow as she bustled from the room.

I grabbed the letter from home first.

Dear Gwyneth,
How are you, my darling? We are anxiously awaiting news from the palace. We cannot <u>*wait*</u> *until they start the television broadcast. Winnie and Remy are driving me crazy, asking when it's going to start.*
I hope you are well. I also hope you are behaving yourself.
What's the palace like? What about the queen? What's she like in person? I've always been so curious. And of course, the prince himself? Have you met him? Is he nice? Winnie wants to know if he's as dreamy in real life as he is on TV (her words, not mine).
Lyra came by. You can imagine what she had to say about all this.
Still, she sends her love. She's rooting for you.
We all are, darling.
Write to me soon. It's very hard having you away from home. We miss you.
Love,
Mom

I pressed the letter to my chest. I missed my mother too, which surprised me. At home, I was too busy feeling superior or annoyed to appreciate her very much. I'd write back to her today and tell her I loved her. It was the least I could do.

I snatched the letter from Dallas and opened it next.

Dear Gwyneth,
The televised portion of The Pageant begins today. Would you do me the honor of having the first dinner with me? Tariq has requested that I dine with each of the contestants individually. I asked to begin with you.

Notice I said "with" you, not "on" you, as mouthwatering as you may be.

You promised the goose would see me later. It's later.

If you would do me the honor, please send a note via your maids.

I look forward to hearing from you.

Sincerely,

Your Dallas

I clutched the letter, a confused wave of emotion rising through me. I didn't want to *want* him like this. It tore at me, as did his sense of humor, which I'd never expected.

But you're here. You're here, and you should make the best of it.

I hastily grabbed a paper and pen.

Dear Dallas,

I accept your invitation. As you said, I promised, and I don't break my promises.

As long as dinner isn't me, I'm happy to join you.

Sincerely,

Gwyneth

PS: Will you see Eve today? How is she?

I folded the letter and carefully put it into the envelope.

Then I spent the rest of the morning wondering just what the hell I'd gotten myself into.

CHAPTER 17
ON THE SPOT

We decided to save the red dress for my dinner date with the prince.

My maids were positively beside themselves about his invitation. With a mixture of excitement and nerves thrumming through me, I felt positively sick. Still, I put on a brave face as they dressed me in a violet gown and fussed over my makeup, getting me ready for my day of lessons and cameras.

I descended the stairs, feeling as though I were walking the plank.

I wasn't the only one on edge. The salon buzzed with nervous energy. Tariq fidgeted at the front of the room, impatiently waiting for us to settle into our seats.

"Ladies, this is the day we've all been waiting for. The Pageant will begin its televised portion today. Mira Kinney is here with her crew. They're setting up in the formal salon. She will be observing us and filming around the clock. But don't worry. I will have final say over anything that's put on television."

A girl with long dreadlocks raised her hand. "Sir? The broadcast won't be live?"

"No." Relieved murmurs rippled through the room. "There will be a live portion, but that's not until later. No need to worry about it for the moment. That being said, you need to be camera ready today. I know your maids dressed you with special care. Mira will want each of you for meet-and-greets. Footage of you interacting with each other and the prince will be filmed as well."

Tariq clasped his hands behind his back. "Remember your goal—to make the public fall in love with you, as well as the prince. The more supporters you have, the better your chances of advancing in the Pageant."

Everyone chattered with excitement. Had they all forgotten what happened to Eve so quickly?

All I felt was worried. The good news was that the broadcast wouldn't be live. The bad news was that the cameras were here, and I wouldn't be able to escape them. In fact, I was supposed to woo the audience at home.

I swallowed hard. I had a bad feeling about this.

Wooing wasn't exactly my thing.

EVENTUALLY, WE WERE TAKEN TO THE FORMAL SALON. THE television production crew was all intense action, busily setting up their equipment and rearranging the furniture.

Mira Kinney was absolutely stunning in person. In other breaking news, she was also a vampire. All the sunscreen in the world couldn't keep your skin that unearthly white.

She seemed impervious to the fact that we were humans. Like Dallas, she seemed comfortable around our kind. Professional and focused, Mira worked with her team to set up camera angles, arrange the proper amount of lighting, and organize an interview list. She checked her notes methodically and frequently.

"She's quite serious, isn't she?" Shaye asked, watching her.

Tamara, another contestant, nodded. "They said she's been working since first thing this morning and hasn't taken a break. No wonder she's so successful. I just hope she's as nice in person as she seems on TV. And I hope she's…like the prince. Civilized, I mean."

Tamara was from Settlement 11, one of the richer settlements. She mostly kept to herself. She was tall, with long raven hair that bounced when she walked. She had enviable physical assets, such as large blue eyes framed by eyelashes that Tariq must have envied, perfect, perky breasts, and a round butt that she must have maintained by doing a thousand zillion squats per day. She wore a floor-length deep-teal sheath that hid nothing and showed off everything.

I wasn't sure, but I might not like her.

"She seems fine being around all of us. But having cameras will be interesting, that's for sure." Shaye sighed.

Shaye had told me that the other girls had been busy forming cliques and making predictions about who would advance to the next round. Wrapped up in my own issues, worrying about Eve and trying to figure the prince out, I hadn't given the other girls much notice. But Shaye said they talked about me, so I would probably have to pay attention to them soon.

"Speaking of interesting," Tamara said, "I heard the prince will begin his individual dinners tonight. Each night, he'll ask one of us to dine with him in a private dining room. Can you believe it?" She fanned herself.

Shaye played with her curls. "I wonder who he'll ask first?"

"Miss West." Tariq interrupted us with a bow. "I have a letter for you."

He handed it to me, and I blushed as I saw Dallas's distinctive scrawl across the front.

"Well, open it," Tariq commanded.

Inwardly cursing him, I opened the envelope as Tamara and Shaye watched curiously.

Dear Gwyn,
I will see you at six. I look forward to it.
I'm with Eve right now. She's doing well and says, in her words, "Hey, you bootlicking East-Ender."
This will require some explaining.
See you this evening.
Dallas

Tariq watched me with glittering eyes. "What did it say?"

I swallowed hard. I might as well tell them now. It was going to get out anyway. "The prince has asked me to dine with him tonight."

Tamara looked me up and down, as if trying to figure out why.

"Good for you." Shaye said it encouragingly, but her cheeks flushed.

"Interesting choice." Tariq arched an eyebrow.

And I just stood there, wishing the floor would swallow me up.

Instead, a harried-looking production assistant came over. She checked her clipboard and peered at us. "Miss Iman?"

Shaye nodded. "That's me."

"Great. You're up first." The assistant leaned forward and pulled down her glasses a bit. "Mira will have my head if I don't get you on camera in five. Let's move it, please!"

Tamara watched as the assistant hustled Shaye off. "She means business, I guess."

"She's the best for a reason." Tariq turned to me, sizing me up. "Do you have a special dress for this evening?"

Tamara inched closer, listening.

"Y-yes. My maids had a dress designed for me because of the broadcast. I'll wear it tonight."

Tariq winked. "Good idea. I can't wait to hear all the juicy details."

I swallowed hard. "Juicy" made me think of steak. "Steak" made me think of delicious. "Delicious" made me think of eating.

What would Dallas be thinking of, tonight?

Tariq noticed my discomfort and tsked. "There, there. You'll be fine. It's not as though you haven't already spent private time with His Highness."

Now Tamara *really* gave me the once-over. I willed Tariq to shut up. I was relieved to see the harried production assistant heading our way again.

"Miss West?" she asked. "You're next."

"See ya." I grinned at Tariq. Even being interviewed by Mira Kinney on television would be better than sticking around here, being sized up, looked down on, and grilled for details.

"Yes, see you." Tariq's gaze followed me across the room as I happily escaped.

"I'M JUST ADDING SOME MORE HIGHLIGHTER HERE." THE MAKEUP artist frowned and dabbed me with yet another brush. "There. That's better."

"What was wrong?"

"Oh, nothing," he said. "It's just your face."

I frowned back, but he glared. "I told you not to move. You'll smudge. Relax your face and stay still. Mira's almost ready for you. She's just about done with Miss Iman."

"Fine." I frowned with my voice, instead.

He ignored me, turning to watch the interview. "Look at her." He sighed. "That girl's sheer perfection."

I glanced over to where Mira was interviewing Shaye, who admittedly looked flawless and stunning, even under the blitzkrieg lights. She chatted easily with the intimidating Mira, and again, I tried to keep the jealousy about my friend's effortless charm at bay.

In my heart, I was rooting for Shaye. But I also knew that she was prettier than me, smarter than me, and a lot less clumsy and ill-tempered than I was.

If I were the prince, I'd fall for Shaye in a heartbeat.

I needed to accept that I was holding on to a little ambivalence about my friend. I wanted her to do well, but *I* also wanted to do well. Still, my friendship with her came before my ambitions, and I would just have to keep reminding myself of that when I felt a stab of jealousy.

Mira Kinney laughed at something Shaye said. *Oh, would she stop being such a suck-up? Sheesh!*

I cursed under my breath. *Note to self—you're doing it again.*

The makeup artist swiped me with his brush one final time. "There. My work is done. You look as good as you can."

"Uh, thanks." Except I was pretty sure he didn't mean it as a compliment.

Shaye and Mira shook hands, and then Mira checked her list. "Next up, Gwyneth West of Settlement Four. I'm ready for you!"

I took a deep breath and headed over. Mira sized me up

quickly then firmly planted a smile on her face. "It's a pleasure, Gwyn. Please have a seat."

"Thank you." I sank into the seat and noticed that I was already sweating. *Great.*

Mira checked her notes. "I understand that the other young woman from your settlement was already eliminated from the contest."

"That's right." I swallowed hard.

"Was that difficult for you? Being the one left behind?"

I nodded. "I think I have some survivor's guilt."

Mira frowned. "That's an interesting way to put it." Up close, she was even more beautiful. Her skin was luminescent and poreless, and her blue eyes sparkled with intelligence and acute attention to the details surrounding her.

She wouldn't miss a trick.

"I just—I just want to represent my settlement well." I smiled at Mira, putting on my game face. "Settlement Four deserves a real chance at winning."

"You're here to win?"

I nodded. "Yes. Absolutely."

"Good for you. I like a strong young woman, and I'm sure the settlements will too." Mira smiled approvingly. "One of the things I'm hoping to do in my coverage of the Pageant is educate our viewers about each of the settlements. How would you describe Four?"

I cleared my throat and sat up straight, knowing I represented not only my settlement but my family. "Everyone is very hardworking, and we look out for each other. Settlement Four is a great place to live."

Mira beamed at me. "That's lovely to hear, Gwyn. I imagine palace life is different than what you're used to."

"Quite." I smiled again. Then, remembering what I was

here to do, I said, "It's lovely. The royal family has been very welcoming." I lied, and I did it with a smile.

Lying was easier than I thought. All I had to do was picture Winnie and Remy starving to death.

"What's the best part?" Mira asked.

"The food," I said immediately. "I had the best popover of my life yesterday."

Mira chuckled. "I'll have to check those out while I'm here. Now, what about the prince? What's he like?"

"He's very tall," I said.

Mira waited a beat. "And?"

I thought of the note he'd just sent me, still in my pocket. I thought of how he was hanging out with Eve, trying to help.

I smiled. "And he's very kind."

"Ah. Sounds like you have a crush."

I reddened.

"Cut," Mira said to the photographer. She turned back to me. "I have everything I need. You did very well, Gwyn. I'm impressed. I look forward to watching your star rise."

"Thank you." My blush deepened as I rose.

Mira checked a note and motioned for me to stop. "You have the first dinner with the prince tonight?"

"Yes, ma'am."

She flashed a megawatt smile. "I'm looking forward to filming it."

I fake-smiled so hard my face hurt. "Great."

As if I wasn't nervous enough already!

CHAPTER 18
THERE'S A POSSIBILITY

AFTER A LONG DAY IN THE FORMAL SALON, I ANXIOUSLY HEADED to my room. I closed the door behind me, grateful to be alone.

At least in here, I didn't have to pretend. I could be a nervous wreck all I liked without worrying about Shaye or Tamara or worse—Mira Kinney filming Dallas and me tonight.

I paced the length of my room, then went and stood by the window. I hoped staring at the grounds for a few minutes might calm me down.

But Dallas was out there, walking with one of the other girls. I narrowed my eyes, trying to tell which one. The young woman wore a stylish, wide-brimmed hat and a powder-blue gown. She walked arm-in-arm with the prince, deep in conversation.

As they turned the corner, my heart lightened. It was Eve. Her hair was tucked beneath the hat, but I caught a glimpse of strawberry-blond curls. She and Dallas were talking animatedly. He gestured, as if he were trying to explain something to her.

Eve nodded and smiled, paying close attention. There was nothing romantic in the way they moved together. I hadn't realized I'd been holding my breath until I exhaled, long and relieved.

Oh boy, was I in trouble.

Still, I smiled as I watched them walking and talking. Since that first terrible night, I'd never expected to see Eve alive again. I didn't know what it meant to be a vampire, but she looked good. As they walked together, continuing to talk, she almost looked happy. The fact that Dallas was making such an effort with her made my heart skip.

I'd been too harsh. I'd been a bigot.

I'd judged him without getting to know him, basing everything on fear. But here was the Dark Prince, taking care of my friend.

He was a vampire. But that didn't make him a monster.

With a renewed sense of calm, I went to get ready for our special dinner.

❧

BRIA AND BETTINA TOOK TURNS SMOOTHING MY HAIR WITH A heavy brush. Evangeline fussed over my makeup.

"We have special jewelry for you to wear," Evangeline said as she applied more eyeshadow. "The prince himself sent it."

"Really?" I tried not to squeal.

Evangeline laughed. "Yes, really. Apparently, the set is from the royal vault. It's priceless. Let me get it." She grabbed a large black velvet box from the dressing table.

Bettina winked at me. "Try not to pass out or insult his family while you're wearing their heirlooms."

"Ugh, right." I held my breath as Evangeline opened the box. Inside, enormous diamond teardrop earrings glittered alongside an ornate, exquisite diamond necklace. "Holy crap!"

Evangeline's eyes bugged out at the jewels. "You could certainly say so, miss!"

Bria and Bettina gasped as Evangeline lifted the necklace and secured it around my neck.

Bria smirked. "I'm pretty sure he likes you."

I gulped as I felt the weight of the necklace against my chest. "I don't know what to say."

Bettina got down in my face, giggling. "Nothing insulting! Start with that, miss!"

Evangeline fastened the earrings and put the final touches on my lip gloss. "There. Now, let's have a look before the prince gets here in his tux, and we all officially lose our minds."

I stood, taking a deep breath, and faced the mirror. The red gown fit snugly up top, accentuating my curves. The bottom of the dress billowed out behind me. The embroidery and jewelry sparkled in the light, making me feel like…a princess.

I swallowed hard.

Bettina put a hand over her heart. "You're a vision, miss."

Bria sighed. "Absolutely stunning."

Evangeline grinned. "The seamstresses outdid themselves."

I collected myself and grinned back. "The dress is lovely, the jewels are lovely, everything's perfect. Now I just need to not screw it up!"

"You'll be fine." Evangeline beamed.

There was a knock at the door, and the maids clapped their hands together then ran for their station along the entryway. "Come in, Your Highness."

A sentinel opened the door, and Dallas strode in, exquisite in a black tuxedo. His hair was tall and tousled, as if he'd made an extra effort with it. "Evangeline. Bria. Bettina. Good evening."

They basked in his careful attention, looking very pleased as they curtsied.

He turned and grinned at me widely, his dimple at full wattage.

I grinned back.

"Gwyneth. You look stunning." He bowed deeply.

I curtsied, praying I didn't tip over. When I raised myself back up, I found his gaze raking over me.

I flushed, probably turning as scarlet as my gown.

He held out his hand for me. "Shall we?"

I grasped his hand, electricity zipping through me. "Yes."

Bettina winked at me as we swept through the door.

Dallas pulled me close against him, and I inhaled his heady, marvelous scent. It made my mouth water.

I refused to think that through.

"I saw you with Eve earlier," I said. "How is she?"

He nodded thoughtfully. "I think she's doing well. I was telling her more about what she can expect in the coming weeks."

"Can you tell *me*?"

"I will train her. You asked yesterday why she was wearing trousers and a tunic. She wishes to become part of our Guard. She wants to fight."

"That sounds like Eve, all right." But I frowned. "Does that mean she'll leave the palace?"

"Not if I can help it," Dallas said. "I believe she's my responsibility. I want to take care of her."

"That's very kind."

"I don't think it's kind, Gwyn. I'm trying to make good on a debt that can never be repaid. I'm the one who invited her here. I should've had my mother under control that evening, but I did nothing. I stood by and watched. That hesitation will be with me forever, on my conscience."

I stopped walking. "I watched you that night. The king forbade you from interfering."

The muscle in his jaw jumped. "I must learn to stand up for what I believe in. Even to the king."

I thought of my own mother and what she could persuade me to do. "It can be difficult."

He frowned. "I agree. But it's worth it. It's part of becoming a leader."

"This world forces it on us sooner rather than later. But that's not a bad thing. I'd rather make my own mistakes, if you know what I mean."

The prince's frown vanished. He took my hands, gently. "I do, indeed."

"Not that I'm a leader—"

"You shouldn't underestimate yourself. You seem quite strong to me and certainly capable of speaking your own mind." His eyes sparkled, and he loomed over me.

Unsure of what to do, I cleared my throat, breaking the moment.

Another genius move, Gwyn! "Thank you."

"You're welcome." He stepped back then resumed leading me down the hall. "But let's talk about tonight. Our dinner will be served in the winter garden."

"Is that outside?"

"No, it's a special room in the house. I think you'll enjoy it. It's one of my favorite parts of the palace."

I nodded. "I'm sure it's lovely. Do you know if the camera crew will be with us, filming?"

Dallas's eyes flashed. "I spoke with Tariq about it, and I laid down some ground rules. They're allowed to film us before dinner, but after that, we are to have complete privacy."

I exhaled, relieved. "Thank you. It's a bit unnerving to have Mira Kinney watching my every move."

"She's not so bad. I've known Mira for years."

"I didn't know she was…a vampire. I could never tell on television."

"Speaking of that." Dallas stopped walking again. "That's something I've been wanting to talk to you about. I'm wondering if we should be more forthcoming with the settlements about our heritage. My father and Tariq are against it, but I feel strongly that the people have a right to know the truth. I think this contest is the perfect venue to bring it up and highlight our similarities, not focus on our differences."

I'd been wondering when, and if, the royal family would let the settlements in on their secret. Now that girls from every settlement in the land were privy to the information, the news would get out. Not even an airtight confidentiality agreement could stop that.

I nodded. "I agree with you one hundred percent. And I admire your bravery."

His forehead furrowed. "Why do you think that's brave?"

For all his sophistication and charm, Dallas seemed a bit clueless about the nature of the people he now governed—*my* people.

I put my hand over his. "The people in the settlements will be afraid, at least at first. Right now, it's just a rumor. No one knows for sure that you're a vampire. Only the people who work for you know the truth." *And maybe the people who went to fight you.*

And Eve. Eve knew.

"But I think telling the truth and showing how you get along with the contestants and treat everyone so well will go a long way to making people less afraid. The more secret your racial identity is, the more frightened people will be."

"Father thinks secrecy is power." Dallas's eyes were dark.

"But let's speak of this later. We're about to be bombarded with cameras."

"Okay. But thank you." I squeezed his hand.

He tilted his chin, gazing down at me. "For what?"

"For asking my opinion."

He leaned forward, and my pulse kicked up. "My pleasure."

He laced his fingers through mine as we headed toward the landing, where Mira and company waited. I composed myself quickly. There were bright lights and multiple cameras set up. I glimpsed Tariq in the crowd of production assistants and sentinels, watching everything carefully.

The production assistants were on us in an instant, fussing over our clothes and hair.

Dallas held on to my hand through it all. "If that man comes near me again with the makeup brush, you might get to see my fangs."

I giggled, even though the thought made me nervous.

Finally, they finished with us. Then the eternally-frazzled production assistant with the glasses took us to stand on an *x* taped to the floor. "Cameras are rolling in three, two, one." She ducked out of the way.

Mira Kinney was dressed to thrill in a floor-length, tight-fitting sequined dress. She held a microphone and faced the camera. "I'm exhilarated to be here with the prince and his first ever one-on-one date with Miss Gwyneth West from Settlement Four. Your Highness, Miss West, it's so wonderful to see you."

Dallas nodded. "It's lovely to see you, Mira. And I'm honored that Miss West accepted my invitation."

Mira beamed at both of us. "Miss West, you look stunning. How are you feeling tonight?"

I gripped Dallas's hand. "I'm excited. It's an honor to be here."

"I'm sure everyone from Settlement Four at home is thrilled to be watching you." Mira turned back to Dallas. "Your Highness, why did Gwyneth get the first date?"

"Well, as you said, she's stunning." Dallas smiled at me. "But on top of that, Gwyn has shown me that she's kind, smart, and supportive. She is a natural choice for my first real date."

My heart did a somersault. Tariq's jaw dropped.

Mira Kinney's grin got wider. "Now *that's* a compliment. I'm sure you'll all join me in wishing these two a great first date. We'll check in with them later. Stay tuned for all the romantic details!"

They stopped filming, and Mira quickly looked at us, her gaze taking in every detail, including our entwined hands. "You two are cute."

"Thank you," Dallas said smoothly. "Do you think you can give us some peace?"

She winked at him. "I already got the shot inside, and the kitchen staff let us film the food. I'm officially out of your hair for dinner. In other words, your wish is my command."

Dallas chuckled. "I think you stole my line, but that's fine. I'm pleased with the outcome."

Mira's approving gaze flicked to me. "You have every reason to be pleased."

The crew started moving the equipment again, everyone talking and jostling about. Dallas gripped my hand and pulled me away from the hubbub. "Christ, this really is a circus."

"It's your circus. At least you can tell them what to do."

"To an extent." He looked back and nodded to Tariq, who was overseeing the crew as they worked. "Tariq would have me filmed in the shower if he had his way."

I shivered, and it had nothing to do with the cold. "That would probably be a popular episode."

Dallas arched an eyebrow.

Ugh. If I didn't have a ton of lip gloss on, I'd have clapped my hand over my traitorous mouth.

"Thank you, Gwyneth."

I coughed. "You're welcome?"

His chest puffed a bit. "I think I am."

Our accompanying sentinels opened two large doors to another room, and Dallas quickly swept me inside. I sensed he was eager to get away from the bright lights and the prying questions. I know I was.

All thoughts of cameras fell away as soon as we were inside the room, which was warm and inviting, like a summer night.

Dallas watched me, smiling. "This is the winter garden."

I looked up, mouth agape. The ceiling soared into an atrium. Enormous windows showcased a view of all the stars in the heavens. Elegant lanterns blazed with hundreds of candles, giving the room a soft, magic glow. The room was filled with trees and exotic plants. I heard birds chirping inside their depths. Fairy lights lit up the gardens around us.

"I can see why it's your favorite. It's stunning."

"Stunning—yes, that's the right word."

I looked up to find him staring at me.

I flushed but forced myself to hold my head high. Dallas held out his hand, and I took it again, marveling at the garden as he pulled me through to the center of the room, where there was a small, perfect table intimately set for two.

The prince pulled my chair out. "My lady."

I sank down into the chair, and Dallas sat across from me, only flickering candles between us. "The staff did a lovely job organizing all of this." I motioned to the white china and the fairy lights winking all around us.

Dallas nodded. "They did. They're excited about the contest, which makes it fun. They're so thrilled to have some life at the palace."

Two liveried servants poured us water and wine. They brought out small dishes of cheese, olives, and fresh-made crackers and placed them in front of me. Again, my mouth watered.

The prince had a sip of wine and watched me with interest.

"*Can* you eat?" I asked.

Dallas scowled. "I had a friend who was turned. In his human life, he'd been a vegetarian. One holiday, his new girlfriend cooked a turkey, and to be polite, he ate it. He said he threw up several times on his way home." He chuckled. "That's what eating your food would do to me. I could eat it, and it wouldn't kill me, but it would probably make me sick."

"So you *only* drink blood?"

He held up his crystal goblet. "And wine. This Pinot is delicious, by the way. You should try some, but only if you want to."

"No, thank you. My mother and I had alcohol the night before I came here. I'm afraid it didn't sit well with me. Much like your friend and his turkey."

"I wonder if he would've preferred goose." Dallas's shoulder shook with silent laughter.

"You're unbelievable." But in spite of myself, I laughed too. "I can't believe the way you and Eve were making fun of me yesterday."

He shrugged. "I was just trying to make light of the situation. I didn't know what else to do."

"I guess I can appreciate that."

"And *I* can appreciate that you're a good sport." Dallas

leaned forward. "I want to know more about your life. You mentioned your mother. What's your family like? Tell me about them, please."

"We live in Settlement Four, as you know, near the downtown district. Before the war, our neighborhood was considered quite posh. My father worked as a bond trader in the city square. He was a partner at his firm. I attended the private academy." I cleared my throat. "I have two younger siblings, Winnifred and Remy. They're adorable. Winnie has the biggest crush on you. She's so thrilled that I'm here."

"And your parents?"

I put down the cheese and cracker sandwich I'd assembled. "My mother's at home, taking care of my siblings. She's very pleased that I was selected for the competition."

"What about your father?"

I swallowed hard. This was where Tariq needed to do his homework, and he'd failed miserably. "My father and my older brother, Balkyn, fought in the war. I haven't seen them or heard from them in five years." I tried to stay calm, but my lower lip trembled.

Dallas winced. "Oh, Gwyn, I'm so sorry. I had no idea."

"I know." I closed my eyes and shook my head. "I don't know if they're alive anymore. I try not to think about it. It hurts too much."

"I can help you find out."

My eyes snapped open. "You can?"

"Yes." He stood and held his hand out for me. "Come with me."

I motioned to the table. "What about our dinner?"

His eyes flashed. "You don't have to pretend to care about dinner. Trust me, Gwyn. I can find an answer for you."

Breathless, I took his hand.

CHAPTER 19
THE LIST

DALLAS LED ME OUT OF THE WINTER GARDEN AND DOWN THE BACK stairs. He ordered his sentinels to stay put. Together, we traipsed through dark halls underneath the castle.

The prince walked swiftly, with purpose, his hand gripped around mine.

"Are you sure this is all right?" I asked, nervously. The gloomy hallways weren't doing anything to alleviate the growing tightness in my chest.

"Your family's been missing for five years, and you're worried about *me*?"

"I don't want you to get in trouble."

Dallas stopped and held my hands. "I'm the prince. Someone's going to be in trouble, but it won't be me. But I promise you, heads will roll for this."

"What do you mean?"

His eyes flashed in the semi-darkness. "There's a lot you don't know about our decision to take over the settlements, about how and why we're here. I can't share much of it with you, but I'll tell you this—I was too young to rule when we came from the North. That's no longer true, and from now on, we're doing things my way. I will not have innocent people suffering. You poor thing, left with your mother and your younger siblings to care for." He grabbed my hand and stormed down the hallway, cursing under his breath as we went.

"I managed fine." I carefully kept my voice even. "I learned to barter in the local market. I'm the one who kept my family in firewood and food."

Dallas stopped and cursed again. "I meant nothing derogatory about your survival skills. I'm sure you were an excellent provider. You're certainly brave. But the idea of you having to fend for yourself, hawking your family's wares…" He cursed again, and I decided to keep my mouth shut.

My heart thundered in my chest as we continued down the hall.

We finally came to a large metal door with a wheel. Dallas opened the vault. The room was pitch black. Issuing another litany of curses, he grabbed a torch from the hall and looked inside.

When he turned on the lights, I sucked in a deep breath.

The room was lined with books in all colors, shapes, and sizes. "Why is your library in a locked vault?"

He raked a hand through his hair. "It's not a library. It's a list."

I pointed to all the books. "That's one list? A list of…?" But the question died on my lips. "It's their names, isn't it?"

Dallas didn't answer. He went and examined the spines of several books at the far end of the bookcase until he found what he was looking for. He pulled out a volume and flipped through it quickly. "What's your father's name?"

"Christian. And my brother's Balkyn." I clenched my hands into fists as I waited.

Dallas examined several pages, then he stood up and

sighed. "They're not in here. And that's a good thing."

"What does it mean?"

"It means we didn't kill them in combat and they aren't our prisoners."

I took a step back, staggered by the news. "They're alive?"

Dallas came closer, his face etched with worry. "I don't know. These aren't conclusive. But it means that the royal family—my family—hasn't hurt them."

Tears pricked my eyes. "I can't believe it. I don't know what to say. I thought they both died in battle. But does this mean—could it mean—that they're still alive?"

Dallas took another step, then stopped himself. "Yes."

I reached for him. "Thank you."

But he didn't come closer. Instead, he looked devastated as he raked a hand through his hair. "I'm so sorry. I didn't know. This must have been torture for you, coming here."

I swallowed hard. "It was difficult at first." I was torn. I wanted him closer, but what we were talking about forced me to keep my distance.

"I can never make it right, what's happened in the past between our people." Dallas's eyes blazed. "But I promise you, in the years to come, I will do everything in my power to bring peace to the settlements. I will also do everything in my power to find your father and your brother, Gwyneth." He bowed before me.

I was touched by his words. "Thank you."

Standing, he looked as if he wanted to reach for me again but stopped himself. "We should be getting back."

I nodded as he turned off the lights and closed the door. We stood awkwardly in the hall for a moment until I took a deep breath.

I stepped toward him, closing the distance between us. I *needed* to be closer to him. It was a physical ache, a yearning.

"You've given me hope that I didn't dare have." I forced myself to be brave, to speak the truth. "For lots of things."

His face softened. "You continue to surprise me. I've not encountered that before."

"Humans have more potential than we're given credit for." I smiled.

He smiled back. "So do vampires."

"I believe it." I took his hand and laced my fingers through his, and we slowly headed back through the underground passages. I was reluctant to end our evening, but my mind raced, turning the night's events over and over.

Father and Balkyn, alive after all these years… They were out there somewhere. But would I ever see them again?

Dallas frowned when we reached my room. "You never got to eat."

I shook my head. "I'm not hungry."

He chuckled. "I wish I could say the same."

"Oh? Is that because of…" I frowned. "Why is that?"

He sighed, and I could feel his breath on me. It made me tingle. "Because, as I told you, you smell delicious. I can't stop thinking about it. It's intoxicating."

"What would happen if you bit me?" I asked, curiosity getting the better of my judgment.

His face darkened. "*Gwyneth.* You mustn't say such things."

But the floodgates were breached, and the barrage of questions I'd been hoarding tumbled out. "Would I turn into a vampire like Eve? Could you just have a little taste? Would that make you feel better, or only make it worse? Would it hurt me, or would I like it?" I took a step closer, feeling strongly for some reason that I might like it very much.

Dallas stepped back, eyes flashing. "I would *never* pierce your skin, Gwyneth. I don't think I could stop myself if I did.

I'd drain you dry. And I would never hurt you like that or put you in harm's way."

"It wouldn't be putting me in harm's way. It's you touching me. I trust you."

He took a step back. "You shouldn't. You have no idea what I'm capable of."

"I know you wouldn't hurt me." I sighed. "I'm sorry, but I have *so* many questions. I just don't know how this works!"

Dallas's jaw went taut, a sure sign that I'd upset him. "How this works is that you're right. I will never hurt you, nor will I let anyone else hurt you. I will protect you with my life, even from my own kind. Even from myself."

"I didn't mean to make you upset. I'm just curious."

"I'm not upset. But I need to be clear, and you need to understand." He took a step closer, and my heart rate kicked up again. "It's a dangerous time for my family and for those around us. So when I say I will protect you with my life, I mean it. Just as I also mean I will never cause you harm. I could never hurt you, Gwyneth. And I faithfully promise to protect you."

"Is that... Do you..." My breathing was erratic as I tried to gather my thoughts. "Do you say that to all the girls?"

He surprised me by laughing. His big shoulders shook. "I haven't spent any time with the other girls, in case you hadn't noticed. I've been too preoccupied with one girl, the only one I have eyes for."

"I didn't..." *I didn't dare hope.*

As if reading my thoughts, he tapped me under my chin, lifting my gaze to meet his. "That vow of protection is personal to you. And I mean it with my whole heart, just as I meant it when I said I would help you find your family."

My own heart did a somersault. "Thank you."

He smiled. "The pleasure is mine."

With a deep bow, he was gone, his cape trailing behind him down the dark hall.

All that was left was me staring after him.

CHAPTER 20
THE MORNING AFTER

I WOKE THE NEXT MORNING TO THE SUN STREAMING THROUGH THE windows, and for the first time in five years, there was hope in my heart.

My father and Balkyn might be alive. I'd always prayed it was true, but I'd never let myself come so close to believing it.

Dallas will help me. A sense of well-being settled over me. I'd been fending for myself since the war. I'd assumed the role of caretaker for my family, but I hadn't realized how much that weighed on me until I'd come to the palace. Now, with the stipend from the competition, my family would finally have some security.

Now, with the help of the prince, we might finally get our family back together.

I hadn't known I'd needed help until Dallas had given it to me. I felt the weight lifting from my shoulders. Even my guilt and fear about what had happened to Eve—he'd helped to alleviate those dark feelings too.

The Dark Prince had brought some light to my life. He'd given me room to breathe.

I clutched the blanket to my chest, going over the details

from the night before. *I've been too preoccupied with one girl, the only one I have eyes for.*

The hope in my heart fluttered, as if it had wings.

Easy, I warned myself. My heart wanted to soar, but there were still thirty-five other young women here. Last night, I was the prince's first official date.

But today, who was I?

I hopped out of bed, anxious to find out.

EVERY GIRL STARED AT ME AS I MADE MY WAY INTO THE COMMON room. "There she is," said the mean blonde with the braids. "I still don't know why he chose *her*."

Maybe because I'm not a nasty cow, I thought, but I kept it to myself.

I hustled to my regular seat, surprised to find that Tamara had joined us at our table. I looked at Shaye, my eyebrows raised, but she only shrugged.

I'd barely sat down when Tamara started in. "We heard your date went well."

"You did? From who?"

"Tariq told some of the girls. We heard it from them," Shaye said.

"I see." The fact that they'd all been discussing me behind my back wasn't a surprise, but it didn't feel great. I slouched down in my seat and grabbed some cornbread, slathering it with butter.

At least butter made me feel great.

"So?" Shaye's eyes sparkled. "How was it?"

"It was good. Fine, really." It wasn't my place to tell them about the vault and the list. I wanted to, but I needed to ask Dallas's permission first.

Tamara arched an eyebrow. "Is that all you can say about last night—that it was fine?"

I shrugged. "It was very nice. We had dinner in the winter garden, which is like an atrium. I could see the whole night sky with all the stars. We had candlelight dinner and private servants." I neglected to tell them I only ate one cheese and cracker because Dallas had hauled me off to a secret, tomb-like vault to see if my family was still alive.

Tamara leaned forward. "Did he kiss you?"

My face flamed. "No."

"Hmm." She tossed her hair over her shoulder and sat back.

"What does *hmm* mean?"

"Oh, nothing." But Tamara's tone indicated that a lack of kissing meant something, all right.

"Have *you* kissed the prince?" I asked.

She narrowed her eyes. "No. But I haven't had a date with him yet, either."

"Hmm." I selected another piece of cornbread and slathered more butter on it.

Shaye looked between us, then cleared her throat. "Today should be interesting. Tariq has us doing some posture exercise this morning, and Mira Kinney's going to film it." She wrinkled her nose. "Should be a hoot."

"But the good news is that we get to see all the footage they filmed yesterday. Mira Kinney wants to review it with all of us so we have an idea of how we're coming across on camera. Then she's going to give us pointers on how to improve!" Tamara practically bounced in her seat. "I'm really looking forward to my date. I think the review will help me so I can be at my best. I sure hope the prince asks me soon. He won't regret it."

I popped the cornbread into my mouth so I didn't call her a *nasty squat-loving cow prat* like I wanted to.

Shaye winked at me, but I just kept chewing.

TARIQ PINCHED THE BRIDGE OF HIS NOSE. "JUST PUT ONE FOOT IN front of the other, Gwyneth! It's not that difficult!"

My ankles wobbled in the four-inch heels. "It is if you're not used to wearing stilts for shoes."

He watched, his lip curled, as I rounded one of the ridiculous cones he'd set down. *An obstacle course with high heels. Now, I'd seen everything.*

"You have a lot of work to do." Shaking his head in disgust, he moved to work with another girl.

My ankle twisted, and Shaye grabbed my hand. "C'mon, I'll help you."

"There's no help for me," I moaned. I teetered around the next cone. "Why would anyone wear these hideous things?"

Tamara zipped past me on the course, striding elegantly in her spiked heels. "Because they make your butt and legs look good, silly."

I bit back a curse, and Shaye giggled. "Don't let her get to you. She's just used to being the center of attention, I think."

"Why do you like her?"

Shaye shrugged. "You've been preoccupied. I had to hang out with someone. Besides, she's not all bad."

I watched as Tamara flounced past another girl, tossing her hair as she went, her nose stuck up in the air.

I sighed, feeling guilty for neglecting Shaye. "If you say so."

The doors to the room burst open, and Mira Kinney

hustled in, all business. "Ladies, our session this morning had been canceled."

Everyone groaned in disappointment, then started asking why.

Mira motioned with her hands for us to be quiet. "I have an important announcement from the royal family."

The room went silent.

Mira straightened her spine. "There are rebel forces in the area. The royal family has had news that they're on their way here, to the palace."

Tariq whispered urgently to his staff of sentinels while worried murmurs broke out through the contestants.

"The royal family has protocols in place to handle a situation like this. The prince will be here in a moment to explain. In the meantime, I need everyone to remain calm."

But calm was no longer on the menu. The girls broke into groups, whispering, as anxiety rippled palpably through the room.

I overheard snippets of conversation as I wrenched off the high heels.

"What rebels? What on Earth is she talking about?"

"Is the palace under attack?"

"Could it be our families out there? Who are the rebels?"

Shaye listened too, her brow furrowed. "I don't know what's going on. I'm scared."

"It'll be okay. The prince mentioned something about..." *What had he said?* "Something about threats to the settlements."

"Threats to the settlements, or threats to the palace?" Shaye peered out the windows. "Are you totally freaking out right now, or is it just me?"

I bit my lip, mind whirling. "I don't know yet. I want to hear what the prince has to say."

Dallas stormed into the room, surrounded by sentinels.

They were all dressed in combat uniforms. Gone was the courtly, charming prince from last night. This morning, he exuded fury, his face a pale mask, his fists clenched at his side.

"Ladies." He bowed deeply, and we curtsied back.

"I regret to inform you that the palace has to implement security protocols. You will all return to your rooms at once and stay there until further notice. There will be guards stationed outside. Your maids will bring you your meals." His eyes flashed. "I am sorry for the inconvenience and anxiety this may cause. But I can assure you that my team will keep you all safe. But do not leave your chambers under any circumstances. Understood?"

The other girls and I mumbled our assent.

With another stiff, formal bow, the prince left.

I wanted to chase after him and ask a million questions. Who was attacking? How close were they? Would the prince himself be in danger?

Were those *my* people out there, or were the so-called "rebel forces" another group?

My mind whirled as we were marched from the room. I longed for Dallas so I could see him, touch him. I also desperately wanted to find out what was going on, but he was gone.

All I was left with were questions. And fear, forming an icy circle around my heart.

CHAPTER 21
FUEL FOR THE FIRE

I MADE ANOTHER ATTEMPT TO PLEAD WITH THE GUARDS WHO stood outside my door. "I need you to do something for me. I need you to check on my friend."

One of the guards was the young man who'd taken me from my home that first day. He grimaced. "Miss, we've told you—three times, now—our assignment is to stay here and protect you. We're not to leave."

"But the prince would want me to know—"

"I also remember instructing you not to speak to the guards, miss." He frowned. "You've not made much progress in that department."

I put my hand on my hip. "When the prince checks in, tell him I need to speak to him!" I closed the door firmly, just short of slamming it. The guard and this whole situation frustrated me.

I had no idea how Eve was, or if she was safe. Had Dallas forgotten about her in all the commotion? Was she afraid? Was she alone or protected?

Eve wasn't my only concern. I paced the length of my room, fretting. I had no idea what was going on either inside or outside of the palace. Last night, I'd learned that my father and Balkyn could still be alive.

Did that mean they were still fighting?

Could they be part of the "rebel forces" attacking the palace?

I gave up pacing and went to the window, staring out absently at first until my eyes focused on the scene below.

There were guards lined up outside, rows and rows of them, with shields and large guns strapped across their backs. There were shouted instructions coming from down there, but I couldn't make them out. Then Dallas came forward, commanding a chestnut horse, his father riding by his side.

The prince shouted more orders at the guard, then rode ahead.

The soldiers followed the king and the prince, marching in formation.

"No." My voice came out hoarse. Dallas was not only going into battle, he was leading it. *No, no, no.*

I felt sick as I watched the army move forward.

Then, from a wooded part of the grounds, the rebels burst forth. Hundreds of soldiers sprinted for the palace, shooting and screaming.

The guards threw open my door. "Miss! Get down!" They wrenched me away from the window and shoved me to the ground.

"Get your hands off me, and get out of my way!" I fought them, anxious to get back to the window.

"All palace guards! Report to the landing at once!" a voice boomed from the hall, and my two sentinels looked at each other.

"Stay here," the young guard warned me. "We're going to be briefed, then we'll be right back."

They left the room, and I scrambled to the window, my heart in my throat.

The rebels and the palace guard had met in the middle of the grounds.

There were shots and screams. Soldiers from both sides were hit. I saw men from both armies go down. I clapped my hand over my mouth as I searched for the prince. I found him inside the rebel's ranks, fighting for his life.

Dallas was surrounded, his horse rearing up as the rebels fired.

Intent on taking the prince, the rebels surrounding him paid no attention to the king. It was a dangerous mistake.

The king circled behind them then jumped off his horse. He grabbed the nearest soldier, wrenching the gun from his hand. The king snapped the rebel's neck with his bare hands.

I held back a scream as the rebel crumpled to the ground. The king grabbed the next man, exposing his neck, and bit him, sucking him dry as the man's arms flailed.

The other guards caught on to what was happening and turned their guns from the prince to the king. But even as they fired, the king continued to vanquish the rebels. The bullets shook his body, but the king staggered on, feasting on another soldier. And another.

And another.

I could hear the rebels' cries. Some started to retreat. But it was too late.

Dallas climbed down from his horse. They fired shots at him, but like his father, the prince seemed immune to the bullets. He was hit, but he didn't seem injured. He kept moving, and he was *fast*.

I sighed in relief.

But then Dallas grabbed a rebel and snapped his neck back. He leaned back and plunged his fangs into him, draining him as the man convulsed in his grasp.

I barely made it to the bathroom before I was violently sick.

I crawled back to the window, unable to tear my eyes away from the devastation. I didn't know how much time passed as Dallas worked his way through the rebels, quickly and methodically. He ravaged soldier after soldier, sinking his fangs into them and emptying the life from their bodies.

The corpses littered the grounds, empty husks.

The Black Guard followed royals' example—they abandoned their guns and attacked with brute, physical force. They grabbed the soldiers and fed on them. The shrieks from the rebels echoed off the palace, an unearthly, desolate cacophony.

In the blink of an eye, the "battle" had turned into a mass feeding frenzy. Some rebels ran, back toward the woods, while others were being grouped together with their hands up.

But the largest group, by far, was the dead. Hundreds of bodies were strewn across the garden, what was left of their blood seeping into the grounds.

One of the royal sentinels started a bonfire. They dragged the bodies to the flames, creating a rebel funeral pyre.

So many dead.

I watched, unable to tear myself away, as the vampires finished desecrating the humans.

When my guards came back, I didn't ask them about Eve. I didn't ask them about anything. Instead, I dragged myself from the window to my bed. I stared at my ceiling. But I was unable to get the image of Dallas out of my head.

Dallas killing another rebel soldier by drinking him dry. Dallas adding another body to the deep pile collecting around him.

Dallas, my Dallas, with the blood of human soldiers dripping down his face as he crushed his enemies.

His enemies.

My people.

CHAPTER 22
THE SHOW MUST GO ON

"MISS?" EVANGELINE OPENED MY DOOR A FRACTION. "MAY I come in?"

"Can I say no?"

She stepped into the room. "Not really. You need to eat something."

"I'm not hungry." My voice was scratchy.

"Please, miss? I brought some tea and toast."

I sniffled but sat up a little. "Is everyone all right? The staff?"

She nodded as she placed the tray on the small table near the fire. "No one from the palace was hurt, except for some of the guards. Three died. Two are in the infirmary but are expected to make it."

"And…the prince?"

"He's fine. He's been in a meeting with his father and the guard all afternoon."

I got up slowly and made my way to the armchair near the fire. "Did you see any of it? The battle?"

But it hadn't been a battle. It had been a bloodbath.

Evangeline's face pinched. "No. But we heard about it."

I took a sip of tea, then shakily set down my cup. "Do you have family out there still?"

"My mother and father still live back in the settlement. They wouldn't come here to work. But I don't have anyone who fought in the war, at least, not anyone close to me." She raised her gaze to meet mine. "I don't know if I could've come here if things were different."

I nodded. "My father and brother fought in the war. I haven't seen them in five years. They never came home."

"I'm so sorry. Today must've been horrible for you." Her gaze flicked to the window. "Watching and wondering."

"The royal guard—they slaughtered the rebels. Barely anyone was left alive."

Evangeline sucked in a breath. "That's what we heard."

"The humans didn't stand a chance. They were clearly outmatched. They didn't even know what hit them. But the prince and the king showed no mercy."

She winced. "But they took prisoners. A dozen of them, I heard."

I shook my head. "They killed *hundreds of people*. In *minutes*, Evangeline. And the bullets didn't stop them." I snapped my mouth closed. I shouldn't be babbling like this. I still couldn't comprehend what I'd seen, but I was putting Evangeline in a bad position by making her my confidant.

"I'm sorry, but I'm exhausted. Thank you for the tea."

She curtsied. "Yes, miss. One last thing."

"Yes?"

She looked at the floor while she delivered the news. "The competition is continuing as scheduled. The prince has a dinner date this evening. Classes will resume in the morning at the normal time."

"What?"

Evangeline blushed. "Tariq said it is of the utmost importance to continue on. He said it's to send the right message to the settlements and also to the rebels. So we're to act as if nothing has happened." Her gaze sought out mine. "All of us —the staff *and* the contestants."

"Tariq is a bloody prat of a douchelord."

Evangeline laughed but quickly disguised it as a cough.

I sighed. "I'm sorry. I shouldn't have said that."

"No worries, my lady. I have to go now, but please ring me if you'd like something more to eat. I'm happy to get it for you."

"Of course."

She left, and I sat there, stewing. Dallas had a date *tonight*?

It was ludicrous that he'd be socializing in a tuxedo, romancing another contestant, after killing dozens of innocent people.

Fuming, I looked outside my room. No guards.

Without thinking it through, I tore down the hall.

❧

I CHECKED THE SALON, THE FORMAL DINING ROOM, AND EVEN THE winter garden.

No Dallas. No date. No film crew.

Where could they be?

Because of the attack, the sentinels paid me no attention. Instead of standing against the walls, per their normal routine, they were monitoring the hallways, watching the windows, and stalking about the perimeter.

They were also all armed.

Lucky for me, they were worried about the rebels, not the girls from the Pageant. So I slipped down another hall, largely unnoticed, determined to catch sight of the prince.

I was in the grand foyer when bright color flashed outside

the entrance of the palace, the deep-blue-teal of a flowing dress. Creeping closer, I got a better look. Dallas stood on the palace steps, his hand securely on the small of Tamara's back. They both smiled at Mira Kinney.

Mira beamed back, then faced the cameras, chattering into her microphone.

I crept closer, careful to make myself small, and watched. Dallas laughed at something Mira asked him. Tamara was all teeth and décolletage, smiling and spilling out of her dress.

It took everything in me to stay inside. I battled with myself. Part of me wanted to go out there and wrench his hand off of her then scream at the top of my lungs directly in his face.

He's a murderer, Gwyn! A monster! And you're freaking out because he's with another girl?

Dallas *was* a monster, a killer. Now I'd seen it myself. Still, white-hot jealousy thrummed through me, making no sense whatsoever, but spiking my blood pressure nonetheless.

The days' events piled up on me, making it difficult to think. My head throbbed.

I wanted justice. I wanted to grab Dallas by the collar and shake him, to cry for what he'd done today, what he'd done to my people and to my heart. Screw the cameras. Screw the contest.

I grabbed the door handle, preparing to hurl myself outside when I heard footsteps. *Crap.* But I cleared my throat and stood up tall. I'd done nothing wrong.

Yet.

"What are you doing down here?" Tariq asked as he came around the corner. He looked me up and down.

"N-nothing. I went for a walk to stretch my legs."

He peered past me to the window and the prince beyond. "Ah. You're snooping."

I raised my chin. "I am not. I happened to glimpse the camera crew, and I wanted to see what all the fuss was about."

"All the fuss, as you call it, is the Pageant. The competition will continue on schedule. The rebels will not be allowed to disrupt what we're doing here. They have tried, and they have failed."

"Wait a minute. They attacked today because of the contest? Is that what you're saying?"

He crossed his arms over his chest. "I am saying that they want their message to get out."

"What message?"

Tariq's gaze held mine. "That they're still out there."

I shook my head. "But they're not out there anymore, except in a pile of ashes."

"There are more of them. They are ruthless. They will use any means necessary to defeat the royal family, including trying to attack the innocent people who live and work at the palace."

"You're saying the *rebels* are the bad guys?" My jaw dropped. "Did you see what happened today? They were massacred!"

Tariq leaned forward, eyes glittering. "I would advise you not to speak about it. Not to the prince, not to the other contestants, not to the staff."

"But everybody already knows—" I spluttered.

"It doesn't matter what they know, or what they think they know. The truth is that the rebels have brought this on themselves. The royals have done everything in their power to make their succession seamless, to bring peace to the settlements. This contest is the latest iteration of that desire. But the rebels want to upend the peace. They want war for war's sake. If you want to blame someone for the bloodbath that happened today, blame the rebels. They've never given the new government a chance."

"Maybe that's because the new government is a bunch of vampires that can mass-murder us in an instant!" I stepped forward. "They can't be killed, Tariq. I saw it for myself today! And they can talk inside our heads and manipulate us! Maybe the rebels don't want to be mind-controlled and feasted on by our new government! Did you ever bloody well think of *that*?"

"Gwyneth."

I turned to find the prince standing inside the door, his face pale, his hands clenched at his sides.

I scowled at him, even as my face burned. "I'm so sorry. I didn't mean to interrupt your date." I spit the words out.

Dallas winced. "We have a production schedule. No matter what else is happening, I have a duty to the young women who've sacrificed to come here."

I suddenly found myself fighting back tears. "What about all the men who sacrificed themselves today?"

His burning gaze met mine. "I did that to protect you. To protect everyone at the palace."

"You did it because you're a—"

"Your Highness, what's taking so long?" Tamara flounced in, her chest heaving, her gauzy teal dress flying out behind her.

She scowled when she saw me. "Don't you have somewhere to be? Like, not on my date?"

"Absolutely." I turned on my heel, fuming, and marched away.

"See her to her room, Tariq," Dallas instructed coldly. "And tell her guards they better start doing their jobs or they're going to find their heads on spikes."

"Absolutely, Your Highness." Tariq caught up with me quickly but waited until we'd left the others out of earshot before he spoke. "You'd best learn to keep your mouth shut, or you're going to be sent home next."

"Good. Please, send me home so I don't have to be surrounded by monsters and hypocrites!"

Tariq stopped on the landing, looking around to make sure no one could hear us. "You are a child. An ignorant, headstrong child. You don't see the big picture, and you don't understand. The show must go on, Gwyneth. We're doing this competition for a reason, a good one. If you keep fighting the prince like this, you're going to find yourself part of the problem, not the solution." His eyes sparkled. "And then you'll be in great company, with more hypocrites and monsters than you could ever imagine."

CHAPTER 23
OUT OF MIND AND OUT OF SIGHT

TARIQ GAVE A BRIEF STATEMENT THE NEXT MORNING AT BREAKFAST. "As you know, the palace was attacked yesterday. It was a fierce battle, but the royal guard prevailed. We are safe and secure once again."

There was a collective sigh of relief in the room, and I wanted to smack the other girls. *Human men—our men—died out there yesterday!*

Tariq continued. "We will be taking extra security precautions. It is crucial that you adhere to your curfew." He shot me a look, which I pretended to not notice.

"One more thing. The rebels want to hurt us, *all* of us. It's of the utmost importance for settlement security purposes that we do not speak of this attack—not to each other, not to our families, not on camera. We cannot add any fuel to the fire. Rest assured that the royal family is taking every step necessary to protect the settlements and stop the rebel forces from hurting more innocent people." He bowed. "I'll see you after breakfast."

I groaned then sat back against my chair. "What do you make of that?" I asked Shaye.

She shook her head, and I noticed there were dark circles under her eyes. "I don't know. But honestly? I don't want to think about what happened yesterday anymore. We're safe, the palace has a plan, and as we're here, on their turf, I think it's best to follow it. Don't you?"

"Absolutely," Tamara said, nodding animatedly. "The prince said he's doing everything in his power to protect us."

I snorted. "Did you see him yesterday? Out on the grounds?"

"I saw him last night, on our one-on-one date. It went even better than I'd hoped," Tamara gushed, ignoring my point and completely changing the conversation so it centered on her favorite topic—herself.

A dreamy look crossed her face. "The prince held the door open for me, he pulled out my chair, he kept his hand on me through the entire televised portion of our date. He's definitely into me. I can tell."

She licked her yogurt spoon, and I wanted to slap her.

Tamara's blue eyes flicked to me, the dreaminess displaced by distaste. "Not even your little sabotage could ruin my evening."

Shaye looked confused. "What do you mean?"

Tamara glared. "Gwyneth was so jealous that she interrupted my date last night. I heard her yelling at the prince. Tariq had to drag her away."

I almost launched myself across the table. "That's a lie."

Tamara leaned forward. "The prince said you're a nuisance and that he only had the first date with you so that he could get it over with. He'll be sending you home shortly."

I sat back, stung, as if she'd slapped me. "Fine with me. Especially after what happened yesterday, with the attack."

"We're aren't supposed to talk about that. So let it go." Shaye kept her voice low, but it was charged with urgency. She turned to the other girl. "And Tamara, you should apologize to Gwyn."

Tamara shrugged, looking pleased at my discomfort. "I'm not the one who said it, so don't shoot the messenger." She finished her yogurt, gloating.

I said nothing for the rest of the morning. I refused to give Tamara the satisfaction. If I was going home, so be it.

After another terrible session of wearing heels and tottering around cones, Mira Kinney came to the rescue. She took us to the formal salon to show us the final, polished version of the first episode.

Mira looked as pulled together as ever, as if nothing had happened yesterday. I felt like I was going crazy. Only hours ago, there were hundreds of dead men in the garden. Yet today, we were practicing walking in high heels and watching a video about a dating contest?

Mira beamed at us. "This episode will air tonight. I think you'll all be pleased with it."

I pictured Winnie and Remy, curled up under their blankets, watching the show tonight, beside themselves with excitement. They didn't know what was really happening. No one did. As the lights dimmed and the large flat-screen flickered to life, I tried to forget about the dead rebels for a few moments.

The royal crest was the first image, accompanied by the settlements' anthem. Then came the royals and a brief, propagandized version of how they'd come to power in the settlements.

The prince had his own segment, during which he declared himself ready for love, commitment, and marriage. Several of the girls sighed.

Next, each one of the contestants was shown. Our names and settlement numbers were broadcast across the screen. I winced when they showed Eve. Her jaunty smile lit up the screen as her strawberry-blond curls brushed her chin.

My picture was taken from my date with the prince. I barely recognized myself in the red gown, my hair tumbling past my shoulders, the large diamond necklace at my throat.

"What is that necklace?" Tamara demanded, but Shaye shushed her, thank goodness.

Mira Kinney narrated the program. "The Pageant was designed by the royal family to bring peace, joy, and excitement to the land. The prince is honored to be able to choose his wife from the young women representing the settlements. He looks forward to joining forces and hearts with one of these special young women. At the close of the competition, he will propose to one lucky winner. When they marry, she will become a princess. One day, one of these young women will ascend the throne and become the queen. She will rule the people of the settlements—*her* people—with the prince at her side. Together, they will bring harmony and prosperity to generations to come."

The next image was of the staff welcoming all of us to the palace. There was nothing about Eve, of course, but the video included the king and queen descending the stairs that first night. The queen's cerulean blue dress glimmered on the screen, and I shut my eyes briefly, even though I knew I couldn't ever forget that dress or that terrible night.

The next montage showed the contestants positively gaping at the rooms, the grounds, the food. They showed Shaye eating a chocolate tart and sighing in pure bliss, which made us all laugh.

Tariq was included, as were scenes of us beginning our training. They showed the prince walking around the reflecting pools with several different girls, including Tamara.

She clapped her hands together when she saw herself, the insipid cow.

"The young ladies have trained in etiquette, academics, and social expectations," Mira narrated. Images of the first girls sent home were shown, including Eve. "After the first fifteen contestants were cut, the contest moved to its next round—one-on-one dates with the prince."

The image cut to Dallas and me, outside the winter garden on the night of our date. We were holding hands, and I had a stupid, eager smile plastered on my face.

On the show, Mira introduced us and asked us a few questions, but I couldn't even listen. My ears were ringing as I watched myself gripping Dallas as if he were the last life preserver on Earth.

And then he spoke. *"Gwyn's shown me that she's kind, smart, and supportive. She was a natural choice for my first real date."*

I glanced at Tamara, remembering what she'd declared at breakfast. She watched the screen, a deep scowl on her face.

Had Dallas simply been putting on a show for me and the cameras?

I was glad for the darkness because a hot blush crept up my cheeks as I grinned like a madwoman on the screen. Dallas said something to Mira, and I watched him. The last part of the scene was us walking into the winter garden together, hand in hand.

I was looking toward the entrance, but Dallas stared at me. In that moment, a look of longing passed across his face.

My heart wrenched.

"Stay tuned for next week's broadcast!" Mira's voiceover said. "More one-on-one dates, more excitement, more romance, and more eliminations. Four weeks to go until the winner is named!"

The screen went dark.

"What did you think, ladies?" Mira asked. "I'm thrilled with the way the episode turned out. I think it has just the right amount of intrigue to really hook the viewers! Now, take a few minutes before you report back to Tariq's boot camp. I look forward to interviewing tonight's lucky one-on-one date!"

Everyone started talking at once. Tamara chatted to a nearby group of girls, telling them all about her date with the prince and opining that next week's episode would be *the best hour of television ever!*

"We'll only be here for four more weeks?" Shaye asked, in a low voice. "I didn't know that. Did you?"

"No. But you heard Tamara. I might be going home sooner than that. Please send me some scones," I moaned.

"Nonsense." Shaye moved closer so no one else could hear us. "Did you see the way the prince looked at you in that video? It seems like he...cares for you."

I grimaced. "I don't think so. If you'd seen him with his hands all over Tamara last night, you'd probably feel the same."

Shaye tilted her chin. "Don't let her get to you. It's a contest, remember? She's trying to psych you out."

"She's doing a good job. Who thinks like that?" She's a... a..." I strung several curses together under my breath, including *cow, prat,* and *squat-loving douche-nozzle.*

Mira Kinney's harried assistant came over, making a beeline for Shaye. "Miss Iman, I've just gotten word. You have the date with the prince tonight. We've sent instructions to your maids that they need to have a special gown for you to wear."

"Thank you, Rose." Shaye was calm and collected, at least in front of me.

Rose smiled. "I'm rooting for you. Pick out something fantastic to wear!"

"Rose, stop chattering and get over here!" Mira snapped from across the room.

Rose hustled off again, practically sprinting across the room, pushing her glasses up on her nose as she went.

Tamara was on us in an instant, all fake smiles for Shaye. "You've got the date tonight?" She wrapped her arms around Shaye and squeezed. "You're going to have so much fun! We had steak. Maybe you'll get to have lobster or something fabulous like that!"

Shaye smiled at her patiently. "I promise to tell you all about the food."

"Ooh, and you must tell me if he touches you." Tamara looked at me pointedly. "If he doesn't, it probably means he doesn't like you."

I stood up. "Where are you going?" Shaye asked.

"I'm excusing myself from Tariq's stupid obstacle course. I'll see you later." I had no right to storm off. In fact, leaving lessons was clearly against the rules.

But as I heard Tamara say something behind my back then giggle, I could give all the flying you-know-whats about the rules.

I needed space.

CHAPTER 24
YOU STOP I START

WITH MY HEAD HELD HIGH, I WALKED THROUGH THE FOYER AND down the hallway to Eve's chambers. If I didn't look guilty, maybe the guards would leave me alone.

The sentinels guarding her door watched me warily as I approached. "No one is allowed inside without the express permission of the prince, my lady."

I arched an eyebrow at him, hoping it somehow lent me the air of authority. "I've been here with the prince before, as you remember. That's tacit evidence of his permission."

The guard winced. "I'm sorry, miss, but he has a list of approved visitors. Your name's not on that list."

I leaned forward, the rage and frustration of the day bubbling over. "I've been in here before. Eve is my friend. After everything that's happened in the past twenty-four hours, I'd like to check on her."

The guards looked at each other but didn't budge.

"Well, this is bloody perfect!" On the verge of a temper tantrum, I almost stomped my foot. "The one friend I have at the palace, and I can't even see her!"

"You don't have to shout, you know." Dallas came up

beside me and frowned. "And please don't harass the guards. They're just doing their job."

"I know that," I said through gritted teeth. "I'm just frustrated."

Dallas gave me a look of mock surprise. "You don't say."

I turned on my heel to stalk off, but he opened the door. "Stop sulking, Gwyn, and come see Eve. She's been asking for you."

I tried to maintain some semblance of dignity, holding my head high as I turned back.

"If it's acceptable to you, I'll chaperone."

"It's not."

He stepped in front of the door. "Then you can't go in."

"Oh, *fine*."

He stepped to the side, and I passed through, holding my breath so I couldn't smell him. Eve stood beneath the chandelier, laughing at me. "Lovers' quarrel?" she asked.

I wanted to hug her, but I wasn't sure if it was safe, and I didn't want to put her in a bad position.

I sighed. "I'm not in the mood to be ridiculed." I went past her and sat on her bed, while Dallas crossed his arms over his chest and lounged against the door, watching us.

"Bad day in human land?" Eve asked. She was wearing trousers and a tunic again, unlike the dress I'd seen her in a few days ago.

"Didn't you hear about the battle yesterday? I wouldn't exactly call it a bad day—it was more like a massacre."

Dallas stiffened, but I ignored him.

Eve tossed her curls, her white skin gleaming in the sunlight that streamed in through the windows. "I heard about it, but the Bully Prince wouldn't let me fight."

"You wouldn't have fought them, anyway. They were humans. Our people. The rebels."

Eve shook her head. "You're wrong. I absolutely would have fought them."

I jumped to my feet. "Has the transformation caused you to lose your mind?"

"No." Eve took a step closer, narrowing her bright-aqua eyes. A zip of fear tingled through me. "Those rebels came here to attack the palace and disrupt the competition. They wanted it to be a big story, how they came and attacked the royal family in their own home. They meant to trap us here and attack us unawares. A coward's plan."

"They came here to fight against the people who took over the settlements and tore our families apart!" I cried. "Those rebels—my father could have been with them. My brother. And the vampires destroyed them all, without hesitation."

"You're wrong about that, Gwyneth." Dallas shook his head. "The rebels that attacked us yesterday are a group we're familiar with. We've fought them before. I've had some of my top strategists tracking your family, and I knew they weren't among the scum who came to slaughter us yesterday."

I winced. "Scum? That's how you view my people?"

"No, that is how I view the group who tried to invade the palace yesterday. That same group has slaughtered innocent women and children in the name of their cause, which by the way is less philanthropic than you might think. They want to rule, they want power, and they want wealth. So I do not call them scum lightly."

Dallas stepped forward, a white-hot fury on his face. "How about your view of *my* people? Mind controllers who would slaughter all of humanity in an instant? Isn't that what you told Tariq?"

"That's not what I said." *Not exactly.*

"I heard you. And to think…" He stepped back.

I swallowed hard.

Eve watched us with interest but smartly kept her mouth shut.

"I should go back to class." My voice was hoarse. "Eve, do you need anything? Are you doing all right?" My attempt to check on her now seemed lame at best.

"I'm fine. I'm doing well." She tilted her chin, her glowing eyes zeroing in on me. "But you don't seem okay."

I shook my head. "Yesterday was a bit of a shock."

She nodded. "I know where you grew up. You haven't been exposed to...what the world is really like. It's cruel, Gwyn. But what Dallas said is the truth. The men who attacked us yesterday were the monsters, not us. I've been learning a lot about what's really happened here in the settlements. It's different than what I believed."

I didn't know what to say. What had happened to my friend who'd hated the vampires? *She's become one of them.* Did that mean she no longer knew right from wrong?

"I really have to go."

Dallas walked with me. "I'll escort you. Tariq will have a fit unless you have a proper excuse."

I nodded, unable to say more.

He was silent as we headed down the hallway, back toward the salon.

My heart beat jaggedly. I wanted to say many things to the prince, and I wanted to say nothing.

Had it only been a few nights ago that he'd held my hand? That my heart had soared with hope?

"I don't have news of your family, not yet." Dallas broke my reverie. "But I have my best men working on it. I should know something soon."

"Thank you." I at least owed him that.

He sighed. "I'm sorry about yesterday. I know you cannot possibly understand."

"You were protecting your people. It was just…it was very brutal, my lord."

The muscle in his jaw jumped. "So we're back to my lord, are we?"

I looked straight ahead. "I'd never seen death before. And I hadn't seen that side of you. I'm still reeling from it."

"I understand." Dallas's voice was grave. "But there's more to the story with this group of rebels."

"I'm listening."

"I can't tell you. It would put you in danger, and that is in direct opposition to my goals."

I started to argue, but several members of the royal guard came around the corner. They marched toward us, leading men in shackles. As we got closer, I could see the prisoners were human, in filthy, bloody clothes—the remaining rebels.

Dallas reached for me and protectively pushed me behind him, shielding me from the mix of sentinels and prisoners.

The soldiers stopped and bowed. "Your Highness, these prisoners have been processed. We're taking them down to the cells."

Dallas nodded. "Make sure they are fed and given warm blankets and clean clothes."

"I don't want anything from you filthy bloodsuckers!" one of the rebels shouted.

The guard nearest to him took out his gun and pressed it against his temple. "Keep your mouth shut! You will not address the prince, and you will not insult the royal family."

"Dallas, please." I reached for his arm. "Please don't hurt him."

Dallas nodded to the guard, who immediately lowered his weapon.

The prisoner sneered at me. "Who's that? One of the sluts who's here to turn on her own kind and marry the prince?"

Dallas moved so fast that I barely saw what was happening. In a flash, he was across the hall. He grabbed the prisoner's neck, lifted him off the ground, and shoved him against the wall.

The rebel's eyes bugged out of his head as Dallas squeezed.

"Don't. You. *Ever.* Speak to her or use that word again in my house. If you do, I'll drain you dry myself. And I'll do it *slowly* so that you piss yourself like the coward you are."

The man turned purple, and Dallas dropped him. He crumpled to the ground, wheezing and clutching his neck.

The prince stepped back and came to my side. Instinctively, I reached for his hand and squeezed it. He gave me a quick, surprised look before nodding to the guards. "Watch them, and keep me informed."

The guards bowed, then helped the wheezing rebel up. They led the prisoners past us, but one of them kept staring at me.

Our eyes caught as he moved past. "Gwyneth?" he asked.

Dallas stepped forward, menacing, but the prisoner raised his hand. "I mean her no harm or disrespect. I know her from Settlement Four. It's been years, though."

I searched his face, trying to recognize him. "Ben? Benjamin Vale?" He'd grown taller and more thickly muscled, and his sandy hair was longer than when I'd last seen him. But his light-blue eyes were the same, and I could see the boy inside the man's face.

"That's right. I was in your brother's grade."

"Have you seen him?" I asked breathlessly.

Ben's gaze flicked to the prince. "No. I'm so sorry. I haven't seen Balkyn in a long time."

The sentinel waiting to bring Ben to the cells looked at Dallas. "My lord?"

"Take him away."

Ben nodded at me one last time, then disappeared with the guard around the corner.

Dallas watched me carefully. "You know that man?"

I nodded. "Not well. He was an acquaintance of my brother's. His family lived in the same area of the city as ours."

The muscle in Dallas's jaw twitched. "I know him, or of him, I should say. He's risen through the rebel ranks, and not because of his courage and valor. He's a vulture. He's part of the extreme rebel leadership. They will do anything to recruit others in an effort to take power."

I stepped away from him, dropping his hand. "I don't know what he is now, but he used to be my brother's friend."

"I want you to stay away from him."

I scoffed. "He's being carted to the dungeon. I don't think you need to worry about us catching up."

"He's dangerous, Gwyneth." Dallas let that sink in. "Stay away from him."

"Yes, *Your Highness*."

He raised his chin, taking my measure. "You wound me, *my lady*."

"Then perhaps we're even," I mumbled.

We kept a firm distance between us as he escorted me back to the salon, both lost in our own thoughts. Mixed feelings jumbled inside me. A boy I'd known growing up had just been led to the dungeon. Another man had just called me a race traitor. My first friend at the palace was not only a vampire, but she seemed to be supporting vampire politics.

My head spun. Dallas had just defended me, and as much as I appreciated it, the damage from recent events still had me reeling. There were so many things between us left unsaid. It was too much to tackle in our remaining walk.

Dallas bowed as we reached the salon. "I'll have a word with Tariq so you won't be punished."

I nodded. "Thank you. For that, and for what you did back there, with the rebel."

His eyes flashed. "You think I'm a monster, but all I want is to protect you."

I wanted to believe him, but I remembered Tamara's words from this morning. *The prince said you're a nuisance.*

So I only nodded in response, unable to speak, fully, painfully aware that I had no idea what I was doing.

CHAPTER 25
RESTLESS

"SO?" TAMARA LEANED FORWARD CONSPIRATORIALLY. "HOW was it?"

Shaye blushed as she buttered her croissant. "It was lovely."

"Did you have lobster?"

Shaye shook her head. "It was some sort of chicken dish—piccata? It had these small green wrinkly things in the sauce. I didn't think I was going to like it, but it was actually delicious."

I cleared my throat. "How was the prince? How was his…mood?"

Tamara frowned at me. "That's a weird thing to ask."

"He was fine," Shaye said smoothly. "He was very pleasant."

"Ooh, you like him." Tamara waggled her eyebrows. "Tell me all the good stuff. Did he put the moves on you?"

Shaye's blush deepened. "Of course not. He was the perfect gentleman."

"Did he kiss you? I bet he kissed you. He *almost* kissed me, but Gwyn swooped in and ruined the moment."

I glared at Tamara. She glared back.

Then the silence stretched out, and my stomach clenched.

"He kissed me…a little." Shaye's face flamed.

"A *little*? What the heck does that mean?" Tamara was still smiling, but now that she'd been outdone, it looked strained.

Shaye shook her head and concentrated on her pastry. "He gave me a brief kiss goodnight. It was over in a moment. It wasn't anything."

Tamara's eyes flashed. "Well, what did he say?"

"He said it was nice to spend time with me. That I was… easy to get along with." Shaye's gaze flicked to me. She looked miserable.

Tamara collected herself. "That's a nice thing to say. I mean, it's not terribly *romantic*, but it's nice."

Shaye shrugged. "Right."

I put on a brave face. "The prince has excellent taste."

Shaye's gaze rose to meet mine. "Thank you."

I smiled. "Of course. You're the one who told me it's better to like him. If you like him, I'm rooting for you."

She smiled back, looking relieved. I couldn't even bring myself to think bad things about her. She was my friend, and she was kind.

And she was certainly easier to get along with than me.

THE NEXT FEW DAYS DRAGGED. WE CONTINUED OUR LESSONS. Mira Kinney and her crew filmed us non-stop—getting dressed, walking in the gardens, playing games during our limited free time. The royals were busy in meetings with their strategists and guards, discussing security and planning god-only-knew what against the rebels.

I rarely saw Dallas. Through gossip, I heard he was continuing his one-on-one dates with the contestants.

There was no word about the rebels or about the prisoners down in the dungeon.

I had a letter from my mother. She raved about the first episode of the Pageant, saying she knew I'd have the first date and *could you believe* how the prince had looked at me.

She said Winnie had gushed about how gorgeous I'd looked, but Remy said I looked like a scary old witch with all that makeup on.

That, at least, made me giggle.

At night, I tossed and turned in my bed, anxious for news of my father and brother. I wondered if Dallas had heard anything. I wished I could see the prince and talk to him, but at the same time, I didn't want to see him at all. There were so many issues dividing us, so many things keeping us apart. And on top of that…

He'd kissed Shaye.

I loved my friend, so it was nothing against her. We continued to talk and laugh and hang out as we'd done since the first day we'd met. But when I was alone, I recognized that I was still choking on a bitter pill—the fact that Dallas had kissed her.

He must prefer her.

The thought pierced me, caused me physical pain. But herein lay the reason I couldn't sleep—what right did I have to be hurt? Why did I care? I'd seen the prince slaughter an army of humans. I'd seen him in his true form—a beast.

I might still try to win the Pageant, but how could I love someone who could do such terrible things?

And of *course*, he preferred Shaye. She would be a magnificent princess—kind to everyone, courteous, beautiful, and smart. If Shaye thought bad things about the prince and the vampires, she had enough tact to bide her time. She would keep the criticism and negativity to herself and discuss things in a mature manner when the time was right.

Dallas had told me from the beginning that he was looking to choose a winner who would be an asset politically, a princess who would help him bring peace to the settlements, prosperity to the land, and get along with his family. Shaye was a much better choice than me. She was kind to everyone and had a level of tact and self-control that I could only dream of.

Even Tamara, with all her flaws, would be a better choice. Her family had connections. She cared about appearances. You wouldn't find her creeping about the halls, yelling that the vampires would kill us all. She had other ways of conducting her business, and you could at least trust her to keep up appearances.

You couldn't count on me for any of those things. Those important things.

So it was settled: I wouldn't choose him, and he wouldn't choose me.

So why on Earth couldn't I sleep?

And when I finally did, why did I dream only of Dallas?

CHAPTER 26
DONE ALL WRONG

The next night proved sleepless as well. After hours of tossing and turning again, I had an idea. I needed to talk to Ben Vale. The idea of him rotting down in the dungeon had been gnawing at me, along with everything else.

And although I had no control over most of what troubled me, I could at least check on Ben and find out more from him. When had he last seen Balkyn? Did he have any news or stories of my family?

I slipped out of bed and dressed in the dark. My guards had been outside my door only sporadically, a fact I'd kept to myself.

I peered outside, holding my breath. No one was there.

I took this as a sign. Whether it was a good or bad one, I didn't know.

I crept down the hall then the stairs. As usual at this hour, I could hear music and voices coming from one of the salons. The king and queen were awake. They ruled the palace at night. It was in my best interest to avoid their detection, so I moved swiftly down the hall, away from the noise.

I encountered no guards. I didn't know what to make of it,

but I was still relieved. Perhaps they'd been repurposed, monitoring the perimeter of the grounds in case of another rebel attack.

I made it to the hallway where I'd last seen the rebel prisoners. The darkness enveloped me as I kept close to the cool, stone wall. I turned the same corner where I'd lost sight of Ben. *This must be the way to the dungeon.*

I swallowed hard, wrapping my cloak tighter around me. It was cold and damp and dark.

Voices were coming down the main hall. I scrambled quickly down the stairs, praying they didn't follow. When they passed by, I breathed a sigh of relief.

I continued down the stairwell. It was lit by occasional torches, but it was still dark, quiet, and cold. The brief feeling of relief fled, replaced by fear. Still, I kept going.

Maybe Ben's seen Balkyn. Maybe he can tell me something —anything.

Two flights down, I saw the landing. There was light down here. *Would there be guards?* I hadn't thought this part through. What could I say to convince them I needed to speak to Ben? What could I say to convince them they shouldn't turn me in for violating curfew?

I reached the landing and, my heart in my throat, peered around the corner. But there was no one. Just an empty stool and a desk with some papers spread across it.

I scanned the ill-lit corridor. There were the cells, a dozen of them, each with bars across the doors. It was quiet, but I could tell I wasn't alone. The rebels were in the cells, sleeping. I heard one snore. I didn't want to wake them or be detected. But I'd come this far. I needed to see if I could speak to Ben.

I crept past the first cell then the next. The men were asleep inside, one flopped on his stomach, one sleeping with his mouth wide open. I stopped when I reached the third cell, almost tripping over myself.

Ben Vale was sitting propped up on his bed, light-blue eyes staring right at me.

"H-hello," I whispered. "I shouldn't be here, but I wanted to talk to you."

He nodded, not at all surprised. "I knew you would. I've been waiting for you, ever since I saw you in the hall." He kept his voice low, careful not to wake the others. "Balkyn's sister would want to know how he was, and I've never met a West who was a coward."

I straightened my spine. "Thank you."

"I lied to you, you know. I've been in close contact with your brother. I just didn't want the prince to hear me."

My heart thudded in my chest. "Is he alive?"

"Yes, he is. I'm *so* glad you're here. You deserve to know the truth." He leaned forward, craning his neck down the hall. "Did anyone see you?"

"No," I said breathlessly. "I wasn't followed. Please tell me about my brother."

He stood and gripped the bars. "Can you get me out of here? It's not safe to talk, not even near the other rebels. I don't know who I can trust anymore, and I don't want to get you into trouble or put Balkyn in any more danger."

"He's in danger?"

Ben nodded. "Grave danger. But it'll be worse if they find out his sister's at the palace. You've got to get me out of here so we can help him."

I nodded, stricken. "Where are the keys?"

"I'm not sure, but the guards usually sit at the desk. Look in the drawers." His gaze burned. "But do it *quickly,* Gwyneth. They could come back at any minute. I don't want you to be caught."

"O-okay." I went to the desk and shakily went through the drawers. My thoughts whirled as I sifted through papers and random office supplies. Finally, in the bottom of the third drawer, I found a metal box. It was filled with various keys.

I showed the box to Ben, hands still shaking.

"Good girl." He nodded. "I never saw the key. You might have to try a few, but that's all right. You can do it."

My hands were clumsy as I gripped the first key and tried it in the lock. *Nothing.*

"It's all right. You'll find it." Ben was upbeat, encouraging, even as I tried three more keys to no avail. "Try again."

I'd never seen so many keys in my life. My hand visibly shook as I tried another, and another.

"It might not be in here." My voice quavered.

"Keep trying." Ben's blue gaze burned. "You can do it. It was fate that I saw you, I know it."

The next key was dark bronze. I prayed silently as I slid it into the lock. I heard a click then turned the key, and the door opened.

Pure exultation broke over Ben's face. He raised both his fists and shook them at the ceiling. *"Yes."*

Then he bolted from the cell. "Come on, then."

I hesitated. "Where are we going?"

"The bloody hell away from here, for starters." Ben motioned for me to follow him down the hall.

"Guards are patrolling the palace and the grounds." I swallowed hard as he started climbing the stairs two at a time.

"We'll deal with it, trust me. Now come on."

I hesitated again, but he'd said he could help my brother. That was what I wanted more than anything.

I ran after him, trying to catch up.

Ben made it to the palace level and flattened himself against the wall, his finger pressed against his lips. Voices drifted past us and continued down the hall. Once they disappeared, I breathed a sigh of relief. "It should be safe to talk here," I whispered. "So please, tell me about Balkyn."

His gaze flicked to me. "I told you, he's alive, and he's in danger."

"But *why*? And when was the last time you saw him?"

"A few weeks ago. But enough about that. We need to get out of here. I'll take you to your brother."

My heart seized. "You know where he is? Right now?"

Ben patted my shoulder and smiled. "Of course, I do. I told you it was fate we found each other."

I shakily smiled back. I wanted to tell Ben we'd make a run for it—the words were on the tip of my tongue—but for a third time, I hesitated.

What would happen to my mother, Remy, and Winnie if I ran away from the palace?

I wanted, with my whole heart, to find Balkyn. If I did, maybe I could find my father, and bring them both home.

But if Balkyn was out there, close enough for Ben to take me to him, why hasn't he reached out?

One thing I knew for sure was that Balkyn and my father loved our family fiercely. They'd do anything for us.

"Are you ready?" Ben asked, still smiling.

"I want to. I want to see my brother more than anything."

"Then let's go." He crouched and peered around the door.

"Ben, I'm so sorry, but I need to think this through. I'm responsible for my family. If I get into trouble, or if I get hurt… I don't know if I can take that risk."

"Fine. And good luck to you." Without another word, he took off around the corner. He didn't give me a backward glance.

I stood there, reeling, alone in the dark.

What do I do now? I'd set a prisoner free, and he was roaming about the palace in the dark, trying to escape.

But soon, I heard shouts in the hall. A gun fired. Ben careened back around the corner, breathing hard.

He grabbed me, shoved a gun against my head, and wrenched me down the hall.

CHAPTER 27
A WASTE OF A YOUNG HEART

"WHAT ARE YOU *DOING*?"

Ben kept his muscled arm around me, hustling me down the hall toward the medical ward. "Getting the hell out of here."

"With a bloody gun to my head?"

He grimaced as I fought him. "Don't make me shoot you right now. Your blood will bring them in droves."

"I thought..." My breath hitched in my throat. "I thought you wanted to help me."

"Well, then you're an idiot, just like your brother."

I tried to elbow him in the gut, but his grip tightened.

Shouts sounded behind us, getting closer. Ben ran, dragging me with him. We rounded the corner and practically ran into two royal guards.

Ben didn't hesitate. Before they could attack, he raised the gun and shot them both in the head. The guards dropped to the ground, and Ben pushed me around them. I looked down. One of the dead men was the young guard who'd come to my house that first day.

Tears streaked my face as Ben dragged me forward.

"I see the humans are acting up again." Eve stepped out from the darkness, her aqua eyes blazing as she took in the dead bodies on the ground, and Ben's death-grip on me. "A bit of a mercenary, eh?"

Ben fired at her.

"Eve!" I shrieked.

The bullet struck her in the chest. It jerked her back a bit, but then she laughed and righted herself. "Not the smartest one, either, I see." She came closer, her glowing eyes focused on Ben. "That's the definition of insanity, isn't it? Doing the same thing over and over again, expecting a different result?"

"Filthy bloodsucker." He shot her again.

"That's exactly what I'm talking about, dude." She grabbed the gun and wrenched it from him. Then she held her hand out for me.

Ben shoved me toward her.

"Are you all right?" she asked.

I hugged her. "I am now."

The guards were closer. I could hear them coming down the hall.

"Do you want me to kill him?" she asked, almost casually.

I glanced at Ben. *Yes,* I thought. "No," I whispered.

Eve stuck the gun into the waist of her pants and smiled at Ben. "I'm going to find out your cell number, buddy. I'm going to come visit you." She closed her eyes.

He put his hands on his temples. "Get out of my head, you freak! Leave me the hell alone!" He shrieked several expletives and fell to his knees, cradling his head in his hands.

I watched as Eve concentrated. She must be saying all manner of things to him. From the way he was rolling around on the ground, Ben didn't seem to be taking it very well.

The guards reached us. Eve opened her eyes and smiled at me. "I'm going to have fun with this. Maybe the prince will let him be my little plaything. I can experiment on him." She winked at Ben, who'd gone white, as though he were about to pass out.

The soldiers raised their guns, all of them aimed at Ben.

"How did he get out?" the nearest guard barked at us.

"I-I let him out." My voice shook. "He said he could tell me about my brother."

The guard pointed to me. "Take her into custody. We'll take her to the king and queen."

"No!" Eve said, stepping in front of me. "She hasn't done anything wrong. This man tricked her. It wasn't her fault."

The guard bowed to Eve. "I'm sorry, my lady, but she has to be reported." He motioned to the guards. "Take the girl. Get the prisoner too. The royal family will want to hear about this."

An armed guard came up next to me, not touching, but not giving me room to run, either.

Eve came with us. "I'm not leaving you alone," she whispered.

My heart leaped with fear. "I don't want you to get in trouble."

"I won't. I'm the queen's favorite, remember?"

I swallowed hard. The last person I wanted to see was the queen.

Eve reached for my hand and squeezed. "It'll be all right."

But as we marched down the hall to the king and queen, I seriously doubted it.

❧

THE MUSIC STOPPED WHEN THE SOLDIERS BROUGHT US TO THE royal salon, an opulent room I'd never seen before. The king and queen sat on their thrones. Their golden crowns gleamed on their heads.

There were other vampires in the room, lords and ladies I'd never seen before. *Did they live here? Did they only come out at night?*

I looked around wildly and caught sight of Dallas. He stood off by himself, near the windows.

When he saw Ben, his face twisted.

When he saw me, he rocked back on his heels.

"Your Majesties." The lead guard bowed. "Three of our guards are dead. I have a team taking care of the bodies."

The king shot up. "What happened?"

"This prisoner escaped and shot them." Two other guards brought Ben forward.

He was still pale, but the hate was clear on his face as he stared back at the king.

"How did he get free?"

I took a shaky step forward. "I freed him, Your Majesty." My voice quavered in the hush of the room.

Eve came and stood next to me, clasping my hand, giving me courage.

"He told me he'd seen my brother. He told me that my brother was in danger and that he could help if I…if I set him free." It sounded ludicrous to me now. *I'd been tricked.*

I shook with fear, miserable and exposed beneath the rapt attention of the king and queen.

The king descended halfway down the stairs, coming closer. "And how does he purport to know your brother?"

I swallowed a lump in my throat. "They were childhood friends, Your Majesty."

A murmur shot through the room.

"Did you free him to help the rebels?" The queen's voice rang out as she joined her husband on the stairs.

My blood turned icy. "N-no, Your Majesty. He said he didn't feel safe telling me about my brother near the other rebels, so I let him out, hoping he could give me news."

The queen arched her eyebrow. "How exactly did you end up in the dungeons in the middle of the night?"

"Enough of this." Dallas shot forward, anger rolling off him in waves. He paced the front of the room, inserting himself between his parents and the rest of us. "I told the prisoners not to speak to anyone here, least of all the contestants who are staying at the palace by invitation, under our protection."

He stopped pacing in front of Ben. "Benjamin Vale, I hereby sentence you to death."

"Dallas—" I reached for him, but in a dark flash of his cape, he had Ben in a death grip.

He stared Ben in the eye. "I told you to stay away from her."

"She came to *me*, bloodsucker." Ben spit in his face. I heard the queen gasp.

Dallas gripped the prisoner, hesitating, and I wanted to reach for him again.

The king stepped closer. "Son?"

The prince nodded, his gaze never leaving Ben's face.

"She wanted to run away—away from the monsters." Ben's eyes sparkled with hate. "Away from *you*."

"Enough!" Dallas roared. He sank his fangs into Ben's neck before he could utter another word. The rebel's arms and legs jerked, his body convulsing, and I had to turn away.

Eve gripped my hand. She was the only thing holding me up.

My eyes were still scrunched closed as I heard the dead body crumple to the ground. Then the silence stretched out.

"Miss West."

I cringed as Dallas said my name, but I turned to look at him.

The prince looked up at me from the ground, where he crouched near Ben's body. He'd already wiped the blood from his face. "I told you *specifically* not to talk to this prisoner. You're in direct violation of my order, *my lady*. Guards, see her to her room, and do *not* leave her unattended. I'll be up to deal with her later. And get this rebel scum out of here. I've seen enough of him for one lifetime."

Eve squeezed my hand one last time before the guards took me away. *They won't hurt you,* she said inside my head.

But as they dragged me away, I no longer cared.

CHAPTER 28
I'M ALONE WITH YOU

"Miss." Evangeline looked pale as she peered at me. "Are you all right?"

I blinked. "Not really."

"I had to fight the guards to get in here. What happened?"

"You don't want to know. Please, go. You shouldn't be near me. I'm in trouble, and I don't want you to be associated with it."

She fussed over me, pulling my blanket up and fluffing my pillows.

"Go, please. I can't have you suffer for my mistakes."

Her face crumpled. "Isn't there anything I can do?"

"No." I rolled away from her, worried her kindness and concern would make me cry. "But thank you for everything you've done. And please tell the twins that too."

"There's no need for all that, miss. I'll be back soon with tea," she said, undeterred. "A nice cup of tea always makes everything seem better."

I doubted it. Would a nice cup of tea make it hurt less when the prince drained me dry?

The door opened again a moment later. "Gwyneth." Dallas

came into the room, then hesitated. "Do you want your maids in the room while I'm here?"

I sat up. "So they can watch you kill me? I don't think so."

He motioned to the guards outside, and they closed the door. Then he stalked to the fire, his back to me, and gripped the mantle.

"Why is it," he asked, "that you hate me so much?"

"I don't hate you." The words tumbled out before I had time to think them through, but I recognized them as the truth. "After everything that's happened, I should. But I don't. I don't think I *can* hate you."

He turned, his eyes sad and dark. "Then why do you do everything in your power to torture me?"

"What? What on Earth do you mean?"

His shoulders sagged. "I tell you to stay in your room. You sneak out. I tell you to stay away from Eve when you're alone. You go to her. I tell you to stay away from one man—*one man*—and you go to him in the middle of the night. Why?"

I stood up from my bed. "Because I wanted to know about my brother."

Dallas crossed his arms over his chest. "I told you I was looking for him."

"You haven't said a word to me."

"I've been *busy*."

"Busy kissing Shaye," I mumbled. I wanted to smack myself. The bodies were piling up around us, and I was acting like a jealous cow.

"I barely kissed her," Dallas said. "And to be honest, Gwyn, I didn't know you cared."

I scoffed. "Well, after you slaughtered a hundred humans and told Tamara that you were eager to send me home, I sort of stopped."

He strung together several colorful expletives under his

breath. "I told you there was more to the story about the rebels. But you didn't listen because you *never* listen."

"I listened to Tamara."

"Jesus, Gwyn!" He raked a hand through his hair, making it stand up in long spikes. "Tamara would just as soon marry a werewolf if it suited her purposes. She's a cheat and a liar, and she's playing you."

I shook my head. "Wait, did you just say *werewolf*?"

He grimaced. "Never mind about that. I came to see if you were all right after what happened."

"No, I am not all right." I took a step toward him, a bit recklessly. "And I thought you were here to deliver my punishment."

I leaned my head to the side, exposing my neck.

The muscle in his jaw jumped. "You really think I'm a monster, don't you?"

"N-no," I stammered, confused. "You just said, in front of your parents, *the king and queen,* that you were coming up here to 'deal' with me. After I set a rebel free, and he killed three of the royal guards, I figured your fangs were the least I deserved."

I fought back tears. I'd as good as killed those guards myself.

"I lied about punishing you in order to protect you," Dallas said, his eyes burning with intensity. "Just like I killed the prisoner to protect you. My parents would never have let you go unless there was some sort of blood sacrifice. Better Benjamin Vale than you. I vowed to protect you with my life. I meant it, Gwyneth. I will always mean it."

I shook my head. "You can't protect me, though. Not from what I've done."

Dallas's face softened a fraction. "It wasn't your fault about the guards. He tricked you. I told you he was trouble. The new rebel leadership is poisoned from the inside."

My chest heaved. "He said he'd seen Balkyn recently. He said he was in danger."

"He *preyed* on you. He's the monster. He put your life in danger." Dallas spat out another curse. "And he deserved what I gave him. He deserved worse."

I shook my head, eyes filling with tears. This was where the prince and I would differ until the end. "No one deserves that."

"That's where you're wrong, and how I know you haven't seen much of the world," Dallas said, sadly. "Some people absolutely deserve to die."

❧

HE LEFT AFTER THAT. I CURLED UP INTO A BALL AND LAY ON MY bed, watching the fire. Tonight, one thing was clear. Dallas had saved me. Again.

But what would tomorrow bring?

Evangeline and the twins brought me tea. They insisted on changing me into my nightgown and brushing my hair.

"There," Bettina said, laying down the brush and smoothing my hair. "Isn't that better?"

I nodded, but I only felt sick.

After they left, I sat by the fire. I watched the flames curl, their different colors bleeding into one another.

I'd made a mess of things. Each time I'd doubted him, Dallas had shown me who he really was.

Yes, he was a killer. He'd never denied that.

Yes, he was a vampire. He had more power than I could ever hope to understand.

But he was also brave and loyal. He'd vowed to protect me,

and he had. From the guards. From Eve. From Tariq. From the rebels. Even from his own parents.

He owed me nothing. And yet, he'd given me so much.

What had I ever given him, besides back talk and disdain?

Tamara had lied to me about what he'd said. And yet, I'd believed her so easily.

Because I'd wanted to believe the bad things about him. Believing the good would mean I was hanging on to hope in my heart, hope that he cared for me, hope that somehow, even though we were from two different worlds, we could somehow...*be.* Hope that he would choose me over the other girls.

After my father and Balkyn had left for the war, I no longer let myself want things. Wanting wasn't something I could afford. It lead only to disappointment.

I'd been right about that. I'd been wrong about so many things, but I'd been right about that.

CHAPTER 29
TAKE ANYTHING YOU WANT

I WOKE AS SOON AS THE SUN BROKE OVER THE HORIZON THE NEXT morning. My maids came in, and I greeted them warmly. I asked for a special dress. Today was a big day.

They dressed me in a red velvet gown, leaving my hair in loose waves. Evangeline attached large sapphire earrings to my ears. Ever loyal, she smiled at me. "You look like a royal."

"Thank you," I said, "for everything."

I descended the stairs and walked to the breakfast room with my head held high. I might be going home today, but I refused to break. I'd learned something important during my time at the palace, and nothing could take it away from me.

"You're looking rather posh." Tamara scanned me up and down. "What's the occasion?"

Of course, she knew nothing about what had transpired last night. "I've decided to start bringing my A game," I informed her.

Her jaw visibly dropped before she composed herself. "Good luck with that."

I didn't answer.

Instead, I greeted Shaye. "How are you, my friend?"

She beamed at me. "I'm well, thank you. You seem rather boisterous this morning. I like it."

"Thank you." I proceeded to eat three scones slathered in butter.

If I was going out, I was going out with a full stomach.

Tariq came in at his usual time. He was pulled together as always, but dark circles lined his eyes. "We'll be practicing dinner party etiquette this morning," he announced and was met with groans.

He looked through the tables, his gaze coming to rest on me. "A word, Miss West."

I stuffed the rest of the scone in my mouth for courage.

He pulled me out into the hall, nostrils flaring as he stared me down. "You brought a load of trouble into my life last night."

"I believe you brought that on yourself. You should have done your homework, Tariq. First Eve, then this. The royals will have your head on a spike before you know it."

He visibly stiffened.

"I don't want that to happen, so I'll continue to voice my support for you with the prince."

He nodded. "Thank you, my lady. The prince does seem partial to you."

"Speaking of His Highness, I'd like you to do me a favor in return for my support."

Tariq looked wary, but he nodded. "Yes, my lady?"

"I'd like you to arrange something for me—a special lunch." I explained the details, telling him exactly what I wanted. "And Tariq? One more thing."

He bowed. "Yes?"

"No more obstacle courses in heels. I've come close enough to dying at the palace. I'm done putting myself in danger."

❧

I WAITED NERVOUSLY, PACING THE ROOM.

Finally, the sentinels opened the doors, and the prince strode through.

"Gwyneth." He bowed, then looked around, surprised. "What's all this?"

I curtsied, then motioned around the winter garden, which sparkled with fairy lights and the sun shining through the atrium windows. "This is me trying to apologize. We never finished our one-on-one date because you wanted to help me. I didn't appreciate what you did—what you've done—for me enough. I wanted to do something nice for you, for once. Instead of torturing you, my lord."

He grinned, and I glimpsed his dimple for the first time in a long time. "I have to admit I'm surprised."

I laughed. "You shouldn't be. I haven't exactly been easy to get along with."

I reached for his hand. "Shall we?" I led him through the garden to the table, which was already set with food for me and wine for him.

I grabbed the wine glasses and handed one to him. "I'd like to toast you. For keeping me alive, despite probably wanting to ring my neck."

The dimple deepened as he cheered. "I vowed to protect you. Even from me." He clinked his goblet against mine and had a sip of wine, then his gaze raked appreciatively over my dress.

My heart hammered in my chest.

"I like it when you're nice," he growled. He reached for my hand and pulled me closer. "It's unusual, but I could certainly get used to it."

My skin flushed. So close to his side, I could smell him, which for some godforsaken reason, made my mouth water.

A sentinel opened the door. "Your Highness, I'm so sorry to interrupt, but the king sends word that he needs you." His gaze flicked to our entwined hands. "My apologies, my lord, but it's urgent."

Dallas nodded. "Of course."

He waited until the sentinel left to turn to me. "I'm sorry, but I have to go."

I smiled at him. "And I am just sorry."

He raised my hand to his lips and kissed it. "Apology accepted."

"For everything?"

He grinned. "I'll have to go back and check my list. It's gotten so long that I can't remember everything on it. I'll see you later, Gwyneth. I'm looking forward to it."

I watched as he strode from the room, cape sailing behind him. Once he closed the door, I fanned myself.

I'm looking forward to it too.

CHAPTER 30
YOU'RE THE ONLY ONE I SEE

Mira Kinney motioned for us to quiet down.

"The prince is away on business for the next few nights," she announced. Everyone started talking, and my heart sank.

"Settle down. He's announced the next round of cuts. Fifteen more girls will be heading home this afternoon, with the same generous stipends promised to the first girls."

Mira pulled an envelope from her pocket. "I have the names. The prince wants you all to know that if you're being sent home, it by no means reflects on you personally. He's had to make difficult choices and has enjoyed getting to know each and every one of you."

Mira opened the envelope and read through the names. The sour blond with the braids burst into tears, so she was going home.

I held my breath as she read down the list. My name wasn't on it.

Neither was Shaye's.

Neither was Tamara's.

The girls who'd been cut gave tearful goodbyes to the rest of us—not to me, of course, because I hadn't bothered to get to know any of them. But as soon as they left the room, the rest of the girls erupted into cheers.

"We made it! We made it!" Tamara jumped up and down. "Only twenty girls left. I can feel the crown on my head!"

I arched an eyebrow at Shaye, and she giggled.

"She's going to be even more difficult to deal with, now that she made the cut," I whispered.

Shaye nodded. "She'll be upping her squat count to two thousand a day."

I giggled. "What about you? Are you happy?"

Shaye nodded. "I am. I want to get to know him better. And I'm not ready to say goodbye to the food. Not yet."

"Let's go beg the kitchen staff for ice cream," I suggested. "Then we can avoid this craziness *and*, you know, ice cream."

"Win-win." Shaye grabbed my hand, and we happily left the hubbub together.

Later, my stomach swollen with too much Black Raspberry, I wrote a letter to my mother, telling her I'd advanced to the next round. She'd be ecstatic, of course. Then I wrote a note to Eve. It seemed silly, as she was only downstairs, but Dallas said he didn't want me going to see her alone. As a goodwill gesture, I was going to listen to him.

Dear Eve,
Thank you for coming to my aid the other night. I don't know what would've happened if you hadn't been there.
I haven't been able to say this, but you seem like you're doing very well. I'm amazed at how you're coping with your transformation.
I hope your training gets to the point, soon, where we can spend some proper time together. I miss you.
I'll come and see you soon.
Sincerely,
Your Bootlicking East-Ender BFF

There was a knock on my door, and Evangeline stuck her pretty face into the room. "You have a letter, miss. From the prince."

"Thank you." I eagerly tore into the envelope as she left the room.

My Dearest Gwyneth,
I'll be traveling for the next week for political purposes. I'm so sorry that I had to leave in the middle of the lovely meeting you'd arranged. I was quite enjoying that dress.
I know they were announcing the young women who'd been cut today. I hope it's okay with you, but I kept you around. I look forward to seeing you—and smelling you—when I get back.
Stay safe. Follow the rules and stay alive, at least until I return.
Sincerely,
Your Dallas

I folded up the letter and went to the window, staring at the garden.

I knew three things.

My want had turned to need.

I'd fallen hard for the prince. The *vampire* prince.

And I had no idea what would happen next.

DEAR READER

Thank you so much for reading this book! It means everything to me!

If you enjoyed *The Pageant,* please consider leaving a review here on Amazon. **Short or long, reviews help other readers find books they'll enjoy. This is a brand-new series, so your review means a lot!**

The next book is coming soon! You can subscribe to my newsletter for new-release notifications:

www.leighwalkerbooks.com

Thank you again. It is THRILLING for me to have you read my book. Please sign up for my newsletter and come along for Dallas and Gwyneth's exciting adventures!

xxoo

Leigh Walker

ALSO BY LEIGH WALKER

The Division Series

Premonition (Book #1)

Intuition (Book #2)

Perception (Book #3)

Divination (Book #4)

Vampire Royals

The Pageant (Book #1)

ABOUT THE AUTHOR

Leigh Walker is a recovering lawyer who loves *Riverdale, Game of Thrones,* and *The Walking Dead*. She lives in New Hampshire with her husband and their three children.

To be notified when the next book goes live, sign up for Leigh's newsletter at https://www.leighwalkerbooks.com/subscribe

www.leighwalkerbooks.com
leigh@leighwalkerbooks.com

ACKNOWLEDGMENTS

Thank you to my readers for joining me! Your support means everything. Readers for the win!

Love to my family, who puts up with me, my blank stares, and my crazy ideas. Love, love, love you. Love for the win!

Thanks to my mom, who always supports and helps me. Moms for the win!

On from all the winning… I need to profusely thank Stephenie Meyer, who has NO IDEA I EXIST but is such an inspiration. I never gave vampires much thought until *Twilight.* It was so much fun to write *The Pageant* and dive into writing about the supernatural!

Continuing in the vein of *Twilight* fan-girling, I listened to the *Breaking Dawn* soundtrack while I wrote this book. Thank you to the artists on the album! I named some of the chapters after song lyrics. The music got *so into* my head, it came out on the page!

The next book is coming soon! I can't wait to share it with you!

That's a lot of exclamation points in a few short paragraphs, lol. But this world gets me excited, and so does the fact that you're coming along for the ride. I'm signing off to write now, but just so you know, I am, forever and truly, **#teamdallas.**

See you in the next book!

xoxo

Leigh

Made in the USA
Las Vegas, NV
05 October 2021